My Name is Toni

Waithîra Francis

- This is a work of fiction. Names, characters, businesses, places, events, locales, and incidents are either the products of the author's imagination or used in a fictitious manner. Any resemblance to actual persons, living or dead, or actual events is purely coincidental.

ISBN: 978-2-9566653-0-4

Cover illustration:
© Evans Mbugua www.evansmbugua.com

Layout and Design
Jane Munjiru pissues@gmail.com

ACKNOWLEDGEMENTS

I'd like to thank the following friends for
the time they took to read, review, and give
suggestions: Darlene Aroko, Laura Trivic, Barbra
Guedes, Mick Flynn and Miriam Wangui.

A special thank you to John Nasaye for helping
me put my thoughts into words. I will forever be
indebted to George Ogutu, Simiyu Barasa and Dr
Eric Mugambi for all the hours they took out of
their busy schedules to edit

"My Name is Toni".

DEDICATION

This book is for my friend Dr Edna Ambundo.
Thank you for believing in me.

And for my son Léni. My reason for living.

Chapter ONE

Toni and Edgar landed in France on the first day of December 1997. The blustery, chilling winter wind at the Toulouse Blagnac Airport seemed to protest their arrival but could not wipe off the smiles from the newly-weds' faces.

The two had been married two months earlier at a colourful ceremony at the Good Shepherd Church in Nairobi, Kenya. On that sunny Saturday morning, over one thousand guests – family and friends – from all over the country came to witness their union. Toni had just graduated from Kenyatta University as a teacher of French while Edgar had just resigned from his job as a tour guide with Abercrombie and Kent, a renowned tour company. Being the good Christian girl that she was, Toni had not wanted to let her parents down by going to France with a man she was not married to. Her parents strongly disapproved of couples who lived together out of wedlock and often spoke about them as if they were carriers of untreatable and infectious diseases.

"These single women have no morals. How can you have a child, yet you don't have a husband?" Her father often wondered aloud.

Something bothered Toni, though: The big wedding photograph that hung in her parents' living room showed a very pregnant bride – proof that her parents had engaged in sex before marriage. She wondered why they were so quick to judge those who were doing what they had done in the past. However, she could not even think of confronting her father, he was short-tempered.

Toni and Edgar's wedding was the culmination of a friendship that started on a Saturday afternoon at the Maasai Market in Nairobi and blossomed into a romance before leading up to a wedding at the church.

On the Saturday of their first meeting, Toni had gone to buy a Maasai necklace for an event at the university's French club. Edgar, on his off day, had passed by his friend's stand to say hello.

"What are you studying?" He had enquired, after Toni said she was a student at Kenyatta University.

"French," Toni had answered proudly.

"*Tu parles français alors*?" He asked.

Toni took a keen interest in the young man at that point, looking at him for the first time. He was a bit chubby, but the dark blue chinos and cream shirt, sleeves rolled up to his elbows, gave him a suave look. He was not tall, but he had smooth skin, a nice smile and very white, even teeth. And, to cap it all, he spoke French.

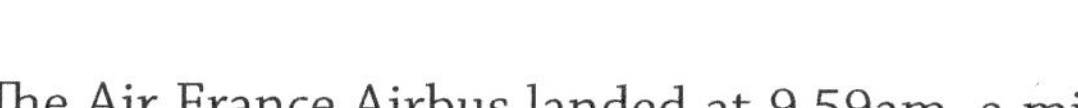

The Air France Airbus landed at 9.59am, a minute ahead of schedule. Toni hadn't really taken the time to find out much about Toulouse. All she knew was that Toulouse, nicknamed

"The Pink City" for its many red-brick buildings, was in the southwest of France, and that it was a student town.

As the ice-cold winter wind howled throughout the airport and its environs, Toni immediately picked up a runny nose. She had had a hard time finding warm clothes in Nairobi. Besides a size too large but warm coat from a friend and a pair of funny-looking mittens she had bought at the Gikomba flea market, Toni had nothing else for the cold weather. As she quickly learnt, the cold weather had been grossly understated.

The Toulouse Blagnac Airport was much bigger and more sophisticated than the Jomo Kenyatta International Airport back in Kenya. Toni and Edgar were amazed at the many brightly lit shops and cafés, which sold all kinds of things, from clothes to souvenirs. It felt more like a shopping centre than an airport. There were many people of all ages and races, shuffling around, dragging suitcases, reading maps, or just sitting on benches, drinking coffee or smoking, probably waiting to pick up their loved ones.

As they waited at the carousel for their suitcases, Edgar remarked, "I hope they didn't lose our luggage. You know, sometimes luggage goes to the wrong destination."

"Really? So, what happens?" Toni asked, surprised.

"You have to wait a few days for it to be re-tracked and brought back to you. I've had to buy underwear for stranded tourists," Edgar laughed.

Toni was full of admiration for her husband. He was eight years her senior and his job as a tour guide had comprised of picking up French tourists who went to Kenya for a safari and accompanying them throughout their stay. In the two years they had dated before getting married, he had invited her several times for lunch at some of the posh hotels in Nairobi such as the Serena hotel, the Safari Park Hotel and the Stanley. He knew all about traveling and even though he had never been out of Kenya, he was more confident than her.

The young couple trailed off towards the bus-stop as soon as they had retrieved their two huge suitcases. They had come to stay for a year and since they did not know anyone in France, they had had to arrange for their own accommodation.

A friend had advised them to join the YMCA, which would allow them to get cheap accommodation at any of their hostels in any part of the world.

"Take the bus up to Jean Jaurès," the receptionist at the airport had instructed in delightful French.

"At Jean Jaurès, take the Metro until Bagatelle. When you get to Bagatelle, ask anyone there to direct you to La rue de Cher. That's the name of the street where the YMCA is located."

"Edgar, do you know what a Metro is?" Toni asked her husband.

"It's an underground train that moves very fast. I read somewhere that the Toulouse Metro is one of the most modern in France and doesn't have a driver."

Toni was bewildered. "So how does it run?"

"It's electric."

It all sounded straightforward and Toni was glad that Edgar spoke good French. She had studied French all the way to university but had never had the chance to practise it. Edgar had spoken French every day at work, so he was very much at ease as his ear was quite familiar with the native French accent.

When the bus reached Jean Jaurès, every passenger alighted. Toni and Edgar fumbled with the heavy suitcases before climbing out of the bus and placing them on the pavement. A few passers-by threw them bewildered looks, which Toni didn't seem to notice at first. When she thought about it a few months later, she realized they must have looked such a strange and funny sight. In France, nobody carries such huge suitcases in a bus. People would take a cab or ask a friend to come and pick them up from the airport.

Toni and Edgar looked around the bus terminus. True to the booklet at the French Cultural Centre in Nairobi, all the buildings around were made from red bricks. The tiles on the roofs were also red.

"I wonder why they call it the pink city and not the red city," Toni mused.

"It's because when you look down at Toulouse from an airplane, it looks pink, not red," Edgar replied.

The open shutters on the windows reminded Toni of the Lego set she had played with as a child. Most of the window panes were white but, unlike Nairobi, they did not come with burglar-proof grilles. A woman at a balcony was puffing away at a cigarette, as she sipped from a miniature porcelain cup, like the ones aunt Susan had once given her to play with.

"Somebody brought these for me from France. They use them for coffee, but I think they're too small for anything," Aunt Susan had said.

"*Excusez-moi Madame, où se trouve le Métro*?" ("Excuse me Madam, where do we catch the Metro?") Edgar asked a middle-aged woman standing nearby.

She responded with a withering glare before going back to turning the pages of her "*Le Monde*" newspaper, her face contorting into a look of disgust. Did she not understand his question? The couple wondered. They decided to ask the next person they could get. A police officer walked by as they glanced around.

"Edgar, ask the cop!" Toni cried, shoving him towards the policeman. The officer burst into laughter as soon as he'd heard the question, throwing the couple into even more confusion.

"*Mais vous êtes presque dedans!* (You're almost inside it!)" he bellowed as soon as he'd recovered from his laughter.

He then pointed towards a big M painted above a door just next to them.

"Let me help you with your suitcase Madam," he offered.

"Come with me."

Toni and Edgar understood why the woman had refused to answer. She must have thought they were playing a silly joke on her, asking a stupid question just to get a rise out of her. She'd simply ignored them, determined to not fall prey to their pranks.

The police officer pressed on a button and the door opened into a lift. He ushered them in and then pressed on "1". A woman's voice announced from an unseen speaker "Minus One" and the lift began to descend. Less than a minute later, the door opened again.

The police officer led them out of the lift to a machine where he showed them how to buy tickets for the Metro and the slot, where they would insert the tickets so as to get past the barrier and into the Metro.

Toni whispered a question to Edgar in Swahili "They don't have a conductor?"

Edgar replied, "No, everything seems to be automatic."

Toni was used to the conductors of the "*matatu*", the most common public transport in Kenya. A *matatu*, a mini-bus or van that is painted in bright colours, has a driver and a conductor whose job is to shout out the destination and collect the fare from the passengers.

At the quay, many people stood waiting in front of a long stretch of glass panes. The Metro rolled in and the glass panes opened automatically. Everybody walked in quickly, but there was no pushing or elbowing, to Toni's surprise.

"Hold onto the rail," instructed the policeman, just before the doors shut and the Metro took off at high speed.

The policeman then pointed at the map that was stuck to the side of the Metro.

"There are sixteen stops from the Balma terminus to the Basso Cambo Terminus. As you can see, Jean Jaurès, where we just took the Metro, is at the centre. You're going to Bagatelle. So, you have eight stops to go. When you hear the announcement 'Next stop is Bagatelle', get ready to alight quickly."

He wished them a wonderful stay in the Pink City and got off at the next stop.

Toni was pleasantly surprised at the treatment. Their last encounter with the police, back in Kenya, had been anything but pleasant: They had been thrown into a cell in Korogocho police station, accused of trespass.

Toni was a student at Kenyatta University at the time. Edgar had promised to teach her how to swim, so they had boarded a *matatu* and headed for the public swimming pool at the Kasarani Sports ground. It was a hot day, made hotter by the distance from the stage to the pool. Toni and Edgar did what everybody else did – they took the short-cut through the fence. There were three ragged-looking men walking towards them. It was scorching hot, but these men wore heavy jackets.

"Hey you! Stop!" one of the men shouted.

At first Toni and Edgar did not realize he was addressing them. Toni looked over her shoulder. There was nobody behind them.

"I'm talking to you two!" One of the men said, pointing at Toni and Edgar. They stopped in their tracks.

"You have just committed trespass and we're arresting you. We're police officers."

Toni didn't believe them.

"Show us your badges!" she demanded.

The men looked drunk and reeked of alcohol. To her surprise, the man who had spoken reached into the inner pocket of his brown leather jacket and produced a police card. His colleague retrieved a pair of handcuffs from his pocket and in a swift move grabbed Toni's wrists and clamped the handcuffs on her.

"We won't handcuff the man. He hasn't said anything. This girl has a very sharp tongue; she needs to be punished."

"Follow us!" the ragged police officer ordered.

Toni looked at the men who were ordering them and what lay in the direction they were heading – long grass and no buildings – and declined.

"I'm not following you! If you want to arrest me, you'll have to fetch a uniformed policeman and an official police vehicle!" Toni spat out.

"*Allez* Toni, *arrête maintenant*," Edgar whispered in French, beseeching her to calm down and follow the police officers. But Toni was having none of it. She refused to budge.

One of the three men broke away from the group, announcing with a sarcastic sneer, "I'm going to fetch a uniformed officer and a Mahindra ... for the princess."

While he was gone, the remaining men mocked Edgar, "What are you doing with this stupid girl? Does she know that we have the power to do anything we want? You should leave her and get yourself a decent girl with good manners."

The police officer returned half an hour later, driving one of the famous navy-blue Mahindra Jeeps with "POLICE" stamped on both sides, a uniformed police officer by his side. As the Jeep left the Kasarani Sports ground for Korogocho Police Station, Toni regretted opening her mouth to ask that the men identify themselves.

Toni had never been in a police cell before. She had read all sorts of scary stories, about stinky cells and of women who got raped in the same cells. As she sat on the cold floor of the cell, which was surprisingly clean and empty, she prayed loudly, in all the languages that she knew.

Edgar was in a separate cell, but she could hear him pleading in Swahili.

"*Afande tafadhali, nahitaji kwenda choo.*" His bladder was full, could they at least let him empty it at the toilet?

After five hours, the shifts changed. Luckily for them, one of the officers in the new shift took pity on them.

"Give me your parents' phone number. The records state that you were carrying bhang," he confided. "If you get summoned to court you could end up in prison for many years."

About thirty minutes later, Toni's parents were at the police station. "Your daughter insulted my police officers! She called them thugs! I'm keeping her here and taking her to court!" Toni heard a booming and threatening voice say.

"Please forgive her sir, I beg you. She will never do it again, please," her mother's unmistakable voice replied.

At the end of it, her parents bribed the police officer in charge of the station with a thousand Kenya shillings to get her and Edgar out of police custody.

As they rode back home in the family car, Toni's father had turned around, and, in a tone of resignation, remarked, "Toni, you need to leave and go to France soon. You've been watching too many movies and you think the police in Kenya are as kind as the ones in Europe. How could you ask the police officer for his ID? Are you crazy?"

Toni did not respond and only looked back at her father with an ashen face, oblivious that her experience with policemen had only just begun.

When Toni and Edgar got to Bagatelle, they were surprised to see many black people on the streets. The area looked quite different from the city centre, where they had only seen a few black faces.

A plump African woman, with short hair and wide hips walked towards them as they stood outside the Metro studying a map. She had a curious look on her face, which quickly turned into a smile.

"Hello, my brother and my sister. You look lost, can I help you?" she asked.

Edgar explained that they were looking for La rue de Cher, the building where the YMCA was located.

"Oh, I'll take you there, it's not very far," she offered.

She seemed incautious, crossing the road without seeming to check either side for an oncoming vehicle, swinging her big buttocks as if she were dancing to some Lingala music. Toni, on the other hand, had quickly clutched Edgar's elbow, never letting go as she scanned the length of the road to assure herself that the coast was clear.

"Why are they driving on the wrong side of the road?" She asked Edgar.

"In France, unlike in Kenya, they drive on the right," Edgar replied.

Toni wondered if she would ever get used to all these new things. As the wheels of their suitcases rolled on the tarmac, the woman informed Toni and Edgar that her name was Laure, and that she was born in Côte d'Ivoire. She seemed genuinely pleased to meet Kenyans in Toulouse.

"There are very few Anglophone Africans in Toulouse," she explained, as she led them along the length of the street. La rue de Cher was only about two hundred metres away and Toni exhaled in relief when they got there. She was frozen from the cold and bone-tired from dragging the heavy suitcase. Her stomach had also launched a series of rumbling protests. She longed for a warm shower and a meal.

"What number did you say it is?" Laure asked, reaching for the piece of paper Edgar held in his hand.

"Number forty-seven," she said, as she looked up and scanned the wall of the building.

"This is forty-five, so it must be the next building," she announced. They walked to the next building, a neat apartment in which no one seemed to live. Toni had expected the YMCA to announce itself with a huge signpost like the Nairobi one. There was a list of names at the door; each name with a corresponding bell. Laure ran her finger up and down the list twice. First, quickly, then slowly.

"I'm sorry, but there doesn't seem to be a YMCA here," Laure announced, shaking her head.

Toni and Edgar exchanged a few oh-shit glances and for a minute, wondered what they were going to do with themselves. Their neat little plan had started coming apart.

Before they could speak, Laure said: "Listen, come over to my place, just down the road. You can store your luggage there as we think of a solution."

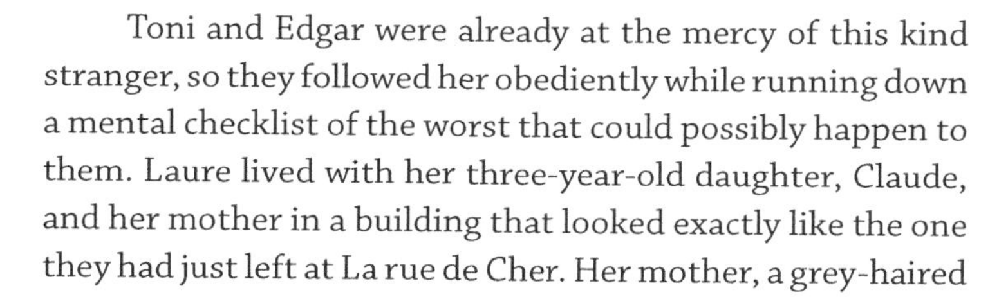

Toni and Edgar were already at the mercy of this kind stranger, so they followed her obediently while running down a mental checklist of the worst that could possibly happen to them. Laure lived with her three-year-old daughter, Claude, and her mother in a building that looked exactly like the one they had just left at La rue de Cher. Her mother, a grey-haired jovial woman, listened keenly as her daughter explained why Edgar and Toni were at their house. She nodded knowingly at each sentence before disappearing into the kitchen to prepare a meal for her unexpected visitors.

Toni asked if she could use the bathroom and Laure pointed to a door down a corridor. There were two unmarked taps at the sink. From visiting the posh hotels that Edgar took her to, Toni knew that the right tap was for hot water while the left one was for cold water. But when she turned the right tap, ice cold water came out; chilling her even further. Everything in France seemed to be the opposite of Kenya.

Laure's mother served them white rice and ox-tail stew that was delicious, but she still apologized, saying that if she had known, she would have prepared a better meal for them. It felt good to have a warm meal after being out in the cold. Toni felt her body revive with every spoonful. Strangely, Laure's mother did not eat with them at the dining table. She took the pot that she had used to cook the rice, put some water in it, sat on the sofa and ate from the cooking pot with her bare hands.

As Laure's mother ate, she spoke to them in a thick, Ivorian accent.

"You can go to the social workers. They'll find you cheap accommodation. They'll give you everything – free food, free detergent, free bus tickets. They'll even give you sheets for the bed. You don't have to worry," she said, as if she had just spoken to the social workers and had already made reservations on their behalf.

She scooped some more groggy rice with her hand and deftly shoved it into her mouth, without dropping a single grain. Toni realized that this woman, who did not know them at all, had sacrificed her lunch for them. She treated them like her own children, yet she had just met them. That evening, Laure asked her cousin Jean to take Toni and Edgar into the city centre and find them a hotel room for the night. They left their suitcases at the house and took the Metro back to the city centre. Toni and Edgar in tow, and desperately trying to catch up, Jean took them through a series of small, winding alleys before stopping in front of "L'Hôtel Splendide". An old woman appeared at the door when he rang the bell and ushered them in with a glassy smile and practised courtesy.

"*Bonsoir Siodame*," she said.

Toni cast a quizzical look at Edgar. "*Siodame*?" What in God's earth did that word mean? She wondered. She would have to look it up in her dictionary, as she had never heard the word before. The old woman gave them keys to a room on the ground floor. Toni and Edgar were too tired and cold to think about food.

The young newlyweds were already broke on their first night in France. A single night at the hotel had cost them half the money they had. They had sold all their wedding presents to pay for their tickets to France. They did not have a single cent kept away as savings and could not count on their parents. They did not know where they would be spending the rest of their stay.

Toni only managed to remove her shoes, before collapsing onto the big hotel bed. She could not believe it. So many years of dreaming and wishing. Things had not started out exactly the way she'd imagined, but that did not matter. She was in the land of her dreams.

Zoning out from both the mental and physical exhaustion, she thought to herself, "Finally, in France."

The Pink City
Photo by David Lagneau

Chapter TWO

Toni's father was a primary school teacher at the Starehe Boys' Centre while her mother worked as a secretary in a law firm in Nairobi. They lived in the school staff quarters with their two children: Toni, who had had just turned four, and Ken, who was a year younger.

On a warm Saturday afternoon in February, Toni's aunt, Susan, and her husband visited with their children: two daughters and two sons. The adults sat outside, basking in the warm sun and enjoying cold sodas and snacks while the children played "Hide and Seek" inside the house.

Wangeci, Toni's cousin, came running to Toni's mother. "Auntie, Toni is lost. We can't find her!"

Toni's mother sipped on her Fanta and answered nonchalantly: "Oh, you know how cheeky Toni is. You'll probably find her in a cupboard. She likes squeezing herself in such small places."

Wangeci ran back into the house and announced to the other children, "Auntie says she's in a drawer." The children started pulling out drawers, opening cupboards, looking under the beds, but they couldn't find Toni.

"Toni, there's a cat in the house!" Wangeci shouted, hoping to scare Toni out of her hiding place. Everybody knew how Toni feared cats. She would jump and scream at the sight of a kitten. But Wangeci's trick did not smoke Toni out of hiding. After a while, the children gave up and left the house for more games outside.

"Wangeci, where's Toni?" Toni's mother asked, in a concerned voice.

"We didn't find her," Wangeci answered, as she ran after one of her brothers.

Toni's mother had looked everywhere for her daughter but to no avail. She turned to her husband and in a more worried tone whispered, "I didn't find Toni."

Nobody had seen her leave the house, and she wasn't in the house either. The adults knocked on all the neighbours' doors, but nobody had seen Toni. Toni was lost.

Toni's father thought fast and went to report to Mr Shaw, a police reservist, who worked at the Starehe Boys' as an administrator. He was known – and feared – all over Kenya, in the 1980s for catching and gunning down dangerous criminals.

Mr Shaw was reading a newspaper when Toni's father knocked on his door. He was always in his office, even on Saturdays.

"Good afternoon Mr Shaw," Toni's father said as he shook the huge man's hand. "My daughter has gone missing. We've looked everywhere for her, but we haven't found her."

Mr Shaw lifted his heavy body out of the chair and came around the desk. He picked up his gun and stuck it into a waist holster.

Mr Shaw and Toni's father then walked back to the staff quarters, about five hundred metres away. As they approached the house, a small girl came running towards them, squealing, "Hi Mr Shaw! I'm not lost anymore! They found me!" Toni's father looked annoyed and embarrassed at the same time.

"We're so sorry for wasting your time Mr Shaw. Toni fell asleep under a huge pile of clothes that our house-help had just picked from the lines," an equally embarrassed Toni's mother explained. Mr Shaw laughed, as he lifted Toni from the ground into his arms.

"You naughty little girl! You really scared your parents, you know," he said in his booming voice.

By the age of five, Toni could read and write. Her father often borrowed books from the library and encouraged Toni to read a story every day.

"I think we should take Toni to primary school, she's bored at nursery school. That's why she's so naughty, "Toni's father said to his wife.

"But they won't take her until she's six," Toni's mother replied.

Undeterred, Toni's father went to see his friend, Mr Kibocha, who was the headmaster at Dr Aggrey's Primary School. They had attended Thogoto Teacher's College together. Mr Kibocha agreed to enroll Toni in Class One before she turned six.

When one walked into Dr Aggrey's Primary School, an acrid smell from the toilets met you from the gate. The toilets were built away from the main building, which held the classes: A simple brick wall partitioned into five cubicles, with doors that didn't lock. The doors were more of semi-barriers for they did not go all the way up the frame. Another wall faced the toilets, with two sinks and taps that rarely let out water. The floor between the toilets and the sink area was cemented, serving as a corridor. The toilets were Turkish-style, which required a child to squat and at the same time hold the door to avoid another child walking in on them. Some of the children would miss the toilet hole and freely relieve themselves on the floors. Others were too pressed or sick to wait for an unoccupied toilet; they did their business in the corridor. Walking around the toilet area was much like playing hop-step jump to avoid the turds of varying degrees of freshness.

There was no toilet paper and some children were too poor to afford any; they would wipe their bums with their bare hands, and then smear the toilet walls with faeces. Toni avoided these toilets and at six years old, had learnt to hold her bladder until it was almost bursting. She would run to the toilet as soon as she got home from school or bang on the door if somebody was using it.

"Hurry up! I'm going to pee on myself!" She would scream as she jumped up and down, kicking at the door until the person inside opened it.

Most of the pupils at Dr Aggrey's Primary School came from the Mathare Valley slums, one of the oldest slums in Africa, where life was survival for the fittest at its best. There was neither electricity nor running water; the "houses" were made of corrugated iron sheets or mud. Raw sewer flowed everywhere, transporting human waste from all over the slums as there were hardly any toilets in the slum.

Every morning, the whole school would gather at the assembly ground. The teacher on duty would lead them in religious choruses that would fill the air as the children sang their hearts out. Toni loved the singing sessions and the songs in vernacular or Swahili. Her favourite song was "Ayubu," a song about Job, from the Bible, who loved God so much that even when Satan took away all his possessions and killed all his children, Job continued to worship God without complaining. Sometimes they sang in English, but most of the children couldn't speak proper English.

Majority of the children came to school barefoot because their parents could not afford to buy them shoes. It saddened Toni to see her best friend, Nyawira, wrap a plastic bag around each foot every time it rained while she walked around in her rain boots from Bata. Nyawira was a fair-skinned girl with short hair and a gap in her front teeth. On the left side of her head was a huge ring-worm that had eaten away most of her hair.

"Mummy, can I give Nyawira some of my old shoes?" Toni asked her mother one evening.

"I don't think Nyawira can fit in your shoes, Toni. You're much smaller than she is," her mother replied.

"I still want to try," Toni said, as she stuffed two pairs

of her old shoes into her school bag for Nyawira to try the next day.

But Nyawira had wide feet that were two sizes too big for Toni's little shoes. Try as she would, the shoes wouldn't fit.

Nyawira rarely carried food to school and when she did, it was *githeri*, a mixture of boiled corn and red beans, in a plastic paper bag. Toni, on the other hand, carried warm pasta and minced meat, or rice and chicken, that her mum had packed in a thermos flask.

All the children ate outside, in the field, sitting on the grass. On the many days Nyawira did not carry packed lunch, Toni gladly shared hers.

Some children carried coins to buy a mango or fried potatoes that a woman sold just outside the school gate. Toni was not allowed to have any money by her parents, but she longed to taste the street food, so she sometimes exchanged her lunch for a raw mango with red chilli and lemon.

After lunch, Toni and Nyawira would join the other children for a game of *Shake*, where members of one team tried to catch members of the other team. *Shake* was played on the unpaved patch of the field, which had a lot of stones and pebbles. Nyawira winced every time her barefoot struck a pebble, sometimes cutting one of her toes, leaving a trail of blood. This made Toni want to cry; she would use her clean handkerchief to wipe her friend's foot. At night, in her bed, she would pray and ask Jesus to make Nyawira's parents richer, so they could buy her shoes.

The classrooms at Dr Aggrey's were simple: a wooden desk with a bench attached to it. There were about forty pupils in each class. One desk sat up to four pupils, instead of two. The children were squeezed and had very little writing space. There were two kinds of teachers: the regular teachers and the trainee teachers.

The trainees wore their own uniform and came every year, from the Thogoto Teacher's College. Toni preferred the trainee to the regular teachers for they were more fun and felt more like "bigger brothers or sisters" than teachers.

They taught the children interesting games and songs. They told them folktales from Africa, about hyenas, elephants, tortoises, and hares. One story about the elephant that asked man for shelter from the rain, for his trunk only, and ended up taking over the whole house, made Toni chuckle.

The regular teachers were a complete opposite of the trainees. They shouted at the children, called them names, pulled their ears and caned them.

Toni's class teacher, Mr Kimani, was the only male teacher in the school. Toni thought he was an old man because, unlike her father, he had white hair. The children feared Mr Kimani because he could throw the blackboard duster all the way to the back of the class without missing the child he intended to hit. He also slapped noisemakers and caned those who had failed a maths exercise or didn't do their homework. His cane had a special name, "Mapenzi".

"Mapenzi would like to greet you, Peter," Mr Kimani would often say to Peter, a boy who never did his homework. His parents were too poor to buy him the text books required. During school hours, his deskmates let him share their books.

"I don't have the textbook, sir," Peter would plead with the teacher, as tears rolled down his face.

"That's not my problem!" Mr Kimani would reply angrily. Peter was so used to the beatings on his buttocks, that he always wore a piece of cardboard in his tattered shorts, to reduce the pain. He screamed in pain as Mr Kimani brought down the cane. The other children who had also not done their homework, winced as they waited for their turn. Girls were caned on the palms of their hands, or on the back of their legs, never on their buttocks.

Toni never failed to do her homework for she had all the required textbooks and her father saw to it that all homework was done to the last minor detail. But Toni was an incurable chatterbox, so she often found herself on the queue for caning.

"You two! Come and greet Mapenzi!" Mr Kimani would shout, pointing at Toni and Nyawira, when he walked into class and found the two girls chatting.

"Please Mr Kimani, we'll never do it again. Please don't beat us," Toni would beg every time. The caning hurt a lot and left the palms so raw that one could not hold their pencil properly, but Toni could not stop chatting.

Mr Kimani also asked the children to kneel in front of the class, for hours. Toni found herself kneeling several times a week for noisemaking.

"Why can't you keep quiet in class, Toni?" Her father often scolded. Sometimes he would be so angry when he saw a comment on her report form, "Hardworking in class but needs to stop chattering."

This anger would result in a beating for Toni. He would get his belt and hit Toni on her palms. Toni would scream hysterically, "Daddy please don't beat me! I promise to stop talking in class."

Her mother would come to her rescue, holding Toni's father's hand and pleading, "Please, that's enough."

Toni's brother, Ken, was her complete opposite. He was never beaten in school or at home, because he was well-behaved and polite. Where Toni often lost her sweater, or her pen, Ken took care of his belongings and always came home clean, unlike Toni who, at the end of a school day, looked like she had been rolling in the dust.

"Mummy, Toni called me maggot," Ken would say to their mother.

"It's not true, he's lying!" Toni would shout even before Ken had finished speaking.

Toni's father would give her a knock on the head with his knuckles and say, angrily, "How many times have we told you to stop calling your brother names?"

"But Mr Kimani calls us that when we're naughty."

Toni's family had two cats, that always stayed outside to catch rats. Because of her phobia for cats, Toni had found a way to keep them away from her – she would throw stones at them and pour water on them. Any time Toni approached them, the cats would run off and hide.

"Toni, if I catch you pouring water on the cats again I'll beat you," her father would threaten.

But Toni always found the time to harass the cats, especially when her parents were away from home.

Toni's mother rarely hit her, and she let her get away with some mischief when her father was not around.

She always threatened "I'll tell Daddy" but she never did. Except the day Toni spat on Phanice, their househelp.

When she was nine, during one of the school holidays, when both her parents were not at home, Toni asked Phanice – a shy girl from the village, who feared her boss – for a favour.

"Phanice, can you pierce my ears?" Toni started.

"I can't Toni. You know your father forbids it. He said you shouldn't pierce your ears until you're an adult," she explained.

"Please Phanice. I want to wear earrings like some girls in school. I'll hide the pierced ears from Daddy," Toni insisted.

Phanice refused to disobey her boss and turned her back to go back to her cleaning chores. Without thinking, Toni spat on her back. When her mother heard what Toni had done, she grabbed the "*mwiko*", the wooden spoon Phanice used to cook "Ugali", (the maizemeal cake that is Kenya's staple diet) and hit Toni on her legs with it. Toni let out a scream as if she were being slaughtered. Her mother also carried out her threat and "told Daddy". Toni's father did what he always did.

"Eat a banana before you choose your belt. I don't beat hungry children," he said as soon as he was told. Toni, shivering in fear, obeyed. After eating her banana in the kitchen, she went into her parents' bedroom and chose a belt from the many that hung behind the door. She always chose the widest belt, because it hurt a little less than the thin ones.

Despite the beatings and her father's refusal, Toni did not give up on her quest for pierced ears.

Every single day, she badgered Phanice.

"Please, pleeeeeeeeze Phaniice, pleeeeeeeze...", pulling at Phanice's dress until the poor girl gave in. Using a heated needle and thread, she pierced Toni's ears. It was very painful, but Toni wanted earrings so badly that she gritted her teeth and did not cry.

That evening, when her father saw her pierced ears, he warned, "If I hear you complain about the pain, or if you get an infection, I will beat you and pull out those threads."

Toni never complained. She dutifully cleaned her ears with hot water and disinfected them with White Spirit, as Phanice had shown her. After a week, they were healed and ready for earrings.

A few months to Toni's ninth birthday, she was done with Class Three. She waved her report form at her father, as she entered the car. "Look Daddy! I am number one!"

Her father always picked her up from school in the evening. It was the second-last day of the school year and Mr Kimani had distributed the report forms for the children to take home.

"Good job Toni!" Her father exclaimed.

Later that evening, when the children and Phanice had gone to bed, Toni's parents sat before their favourite TV programme *"Wrestling,"* holding mugs of tea in their hands. They enjoyed watching the fake fights and each of them had their favourite wrestler. Toni's mother was soaking her feet in a basin of warm water, as she did every evening before going to bed.

"We must transfer Toni from Dr Aggrey's. I compared her work with that of the children at Starehe. Her school is way behind the national programme," Toni's father said to his wife.

"I agree," she replied. "And her English is suffering too. They only speak Swahili and vernacular in that school. Surely, how will they manage when they have to speak to foreigners?"

"It's a pity they don't admit girls in Starehe. Ken will soon have a better education than his sister if we don't move her," Toni's father added.

Ken had gone straight to Starehe after kindergarten. Toni's father looked for a school that wasn't too far away from Starehe but had a good reputation. He also wanted a school which did not require Toni to sit an interview. Even though she was always first at Dr Aggrey's, he wasn't sure she could compete with children from better schools.

One week later, as they were all having dinner, Toni's mother said, "Toni, we have something to tell you."

Phanice had prepared "*chapati*," a flat Indian bread, and beef-stew. It was Toni's father's favourite dish.

"Let her finish her food first," interrupted Toni's father. "You know Toni, she might start chattering and never finish her dinner."

After Phanice had cleared their plates and wiped the table, Toni's mother spoke. "You're moving to a new school. It's called City Primary School and it's much better than Dr Aggrey's."

Toni's eyes filled with tears. "But why Mummy? I love my school, I don't want to move!"

We want you to go to a school where all the children speak English," her father said firmly.

As much as she hated the toilets and the beatings at "Dr Ugly's", as Ken referred to her school, Toni didn't want to change schools. She would miss the Church songs they sang every morning at Assembly. She would miss her friend Nyawira and the kind trainee teachers.

That night when she prayed, Toni was distraught.

"Jesus," she began, "Why did you let my parents change my school? I didn't even get a chance to say goodbye to Nyawira. You're not kind," she prayed as she sobbed into her pillow, her little shoulders heaving with sadness.

Toni quickly forgot about Dr Aggrey's because City Primary School was amazing. All the buildings were painted milk white, and the floors in the classrooms were wooden and polished. The desks were neatly arranged. What is more, each desk was shared by only two pupils. Toni couldn't believe the amount of leg room when she first sat down at her desk. It was so different from Dr Aggrey's!

Near the administration block stood a huge model of a ship enclosed in a glass cabinet, where all the children deposited their snack boxes when they arrived in the morning. City Primary School even had an upstairs! A large, winding staircase led to the top floor and children would rush through the stairs, taking two or three steps at a time. Others would just slide down the side rails when the teachers were not looking. The assembly area was wide and cemented, not dusty like Dr Aggrey's. All the children had shoes that gleamed from the shoe polish and their clothes were neat and ironed. Toni loved the uniform, a chequered red and white dress with a belt, a navy-blue sweater or blazer, white socks, and black shoes. When her parents first took her to "School Outfitters" to buy her new uniform, Toni gaped in awe when the Indian shopkeeper handed her a blazer as part of her school uniform. She thought the man had made a mistake. It was so cool that when they got home, her mother had to put her foot down for Toni to remove the uniform after she'd insisted on "trying it out once again just to make sure it fits."

Chapter THREE

On her first day at City Primary School, Toni was dying to check out the toilets. As soon as the bell for break rang, she ran to the toilets, a rush of sordid pictures filling her head. But when she got there, it was the best discovery she'd made about the school.

The toilets were clean and fresh, not stinky and dark like the ones at Dr Aggrey's. The doors were proper doors, complete with a latch on the inside and the flush worked just like the toilet at home!

She could not believe how different it was and she wondered why somebody couldn't repair the toilets at Dr Aggrey's so that the children there would be happy. Toni wished she could bring Nyawira to her new school.

City Primary was situated in Ngara, an area with a lot of Indian families. During the construction of the East African railway, the British had recruited labourers from India, and some of them had settled in Kenya, around the Ngara and Parklands areas. There were a lot of Indian teachers and pupils in the school. It would be an exciting experience for Toni, who had never met any non-Africans, except Anne-

Marie, Aunt Susan's colleague, who was French.

That morning, the headmaster, Mr Mwangi, had received Toni and her parents. He had shown them where her new class would be, before asking her to join the other children for assembly. After assembly, she had followed the other children to class 4P1, and sat nervously on an empty desk at the front of the class. A beautiful Indian woman walked into the class. Toni wondered who she was. She wore a saree and looked like a queen without her tiara. Her wrists were decorated with what looked like a thousand gold and silver bangles which jingled as she walked. Suddenly the squealing and murmuring died down.

All the children stood up and said in unison: "Good morning Mrs Bakshi!" Then they sat down before Toni could even stand up.

"Hello children!" Mrs Bakshi replied in a singsong voice, as she turned to look at Toni.

"Please welcome Toni, she's a new pupil in the school. Make her feel at home. She will sit next to you, Denis," she instructed, pointing to the empty spot next to a neat boy with glasses. Denis was not happy to have a girl sit next to him; he squirmed and moved to the farthest end of the desk.

Mrs Bakshi spoke with a heavy Indian accent, and at first, Toni could not understand her words. She would say "vy" for "why", "vear" instead of "where", "deks" for "desk" and "fai jiro jiro" instead of "five zero zero".

"Children, please take out your snakes and bring them to my deks," she instructed while her head danced on top of her neck.

Toni almost ran out of the room. Snakes? What kind of

school was this? All the children removed their snack boxes and took them to the front of the class to share with their classmates. Toni was relieved.

Before the week was over, Toni's deskmate Denis had already separated their shared desk.

"There's a line here," he said to Toni, drawing an imaginary line with his finger along the middle of the desk. "You're not supposed to cross it."

"What will you do if I cross it?" Toni asked, rolling her eyes at him.

"I'll beat you on closing day," he spat back.

Toni sneered at him and thought, "What a silly boy."

Denis was also the class monitor with the unenviable task of noting down the noisemakers when Mrs Bakshi was not in the classroom. All the other children feared him, and he couldn't understand why this new girl, who was smaller than most of the other children, didn't seem scared of him. Toni would deliberately put her elbow on Denis's side of the desk and glare at him, daring him to beat her.

He would then whisper, "Please remove your elbow, Toni, I don't have space to write."

He didn't want his friends to know that Toni, who was used to the rough children from Mathare, was not scared of him.

Toni quickly made friends in her class and within a few weeks was always first on the list of noisemakers. After a few weeks, Denis never even bothered to check if she was chatting. When he got to school in the morning, he would pull out his noisemakers' book and note "Toni" next to the number "One". Once he had noted down all the noisemakers, he would begin to add asterisks next to the names, to indicate how many times he'd caught them chatting. Toni's name always had at least ten asterisks by the end of each day. Mrs Bakshi did not cane the children, but she asked them to kneel in front of the class for thirty minutes. One day, Mrs Bakshi walked into the class in a very bad mood and asked for the list of noisemakers from Denis.

"But Denis," Mrs Bakshi screeched, running her eyes up and down the list. "Toni is absent today! She had a doctor's appointment. Vy is she on this list?"

The whole class burst into laughter much to Denis's embarrassment.

One Wednesday lunch break, as Toni and her friend Anne were strolling along the school corridors, they heard children singing from one of the classrooms.

"How come they still have class and it is lunchtime?" Toni asked.

"Oh, that's the French class. There's a French teacher who comes every Wednesday to teach French. I went once, but it was too difficult, so I've never gone back," Anne replied.

Toni's eyes opened wide. Her Aunt Susan, who worked for a French company, took French classes at the Alliance Française and listened to French music. She also traveled to France for work and brought her presents like miniature Tour Eiffel and Chocolate.

Toni was curious; she wanted to try the French class, but she had to wait for the next Wednesday. The French teacher was a tall man whose trousers never touched his shoes, and who always wore the same pair of brown leather shoes. His name was "Teacher Jacques" and he went around primary schools in Nairobi, giving free French lessons at lunchtime.

Toni thought the sound of the French words felt like honey – smooth and sweet – as they rolled off Teacher Jacques's tongue.

Every Wednesday, Toni would gobble up her lunch and run to the French class. She tried to roll the "r" the way Teacher Jacques did, as if it was something between a 'g' and a 'k', with the back of her throat.

Teacher Jacques taught the children the alphabet, how to count, and songs like '*Alouette, gentille alouette*' and '*Sur le pont d'avignon*'. Even though she did not know what the songs were talking about, Toni learnt them by heart and tried to sing them with a perfect accent, like Teacher Jacques. She often talked to herself with the few French words she knew, pretending that someone was addressing her in French.

"Mum, one day I'll go and live in France," Toni announced to her mother, a few months before her tenth birthday.

It was a hot Saturday afternoon and they were sitting on the veranda of their house, enjoying the cool breeze that came in through the open door. Toni's father had taken Ken to the barber's, so Toni and her mother were alone.

Toni's mother was reading *"Facing Mount Kenya"* by Jomo Kenyatta, while Toni had a French story book *"Pierre et Seydou,"* a gift from Aunt Susan, in her hands.

Her mother laughed and said, "That's a good idea, but you first need to learn French properly. I don't think Teacher Jacques's classes are enough. You'd better choose a high school that teaches French," her mother advised.

"Why can't you let me take classes at the Alliance Française on Saturdays?" Toni pushed on.

"It's too expensive for us, Toni."

Toni still had four years of primary school, before she could join high school, but her mind was made up. She wanted to speak French fluently and go to France to live there.

When Toni was ten, in Class Five, something unexpected happened. It was a queer day, which started unsure of itself. The sun peeked out from the clouds then hid every few minutes, as if it wasn't sure it wanted to show itself. The temperatures were cooler than usual, and a strange wind howled between the trees and the tall school buildings.

The pupils had gathered at the assembly ground as usual, chatting and squealing, waiting for the teacher on duty to call them to attention. The routine was the same every morning: the teacher on duty would lead the school in reciting the Loyalty Pledge.

> *"I pledge my loyalty to the President*
> *and Nation of Kenya'*
> *My readiness and duty to*
> *defend the flag of our Republic.*
> *My devotion to the words of*
> *our national anthem..."*

... would fill the air as the children recited like parrots, not knowing what they were pledging and why.

They would then sing the National Anthem, either in English or Swahili, before the headmaster, Mr Mwangi, walked to the podium to address the school. Mr Mwangi was a big man, with very dark skin that shone. He had a loud, booming voice, and he used a lot of gestures when he spoke. He would tell the children about new developments in the school, introduce a new teacher, or scold a class for misbehaviour. Finally, he would wish them a good day and the children would race to their different classrooms to begin the day's lessons.

But something was not right that morning. The sky had darkened as if someone had just dimmed the lights, yet it was only eight o'clock in the morning. There was an eerie silence that did not usually fill the morning assembly. Instead of the teacher on duty, it was the deputy-headmistress, Mrs Wafula, who had walked up to the podium, walking a lot slower than usual, Toni had thought.

Mrs Wafula had removed her glasses and wiped her eyes with a white handkerchief before putting them back on. Her eyes were red and raw, and when she opened her mouth to speak, her voice sounded weak and tired.

"Good morning school," she broke out in a soft strained voice. "I have very bad news to announce to you this morning. Our dear headmaster, Mr Mwangi, is no more. He passed away last night," she said quickly.

"We are releasing you for the day. Please go home directly. Do not stray or linger in the streets. Go home straight and break the news to your parents."

There was a deafening silence as the pupils exchanged shocked glances.

"That's all. Please go home now," she whispered.

Toni's heart sank with sadness as she thought about the words "no more." She'd never heard those words before, and they both frightened and confused her. Did that mean that Mr Mwangi would never come back? How had he passed away? Mrs Wafula hadn't given the children any details. As the thoughts raced in her mind, Toni suddenly realized that she had been standing at the same spot and almost all the children had left.

Like most of the children at City Primary, Toni was dropped off and picked from school by her father every day. She had never gone home alone and had never once used public transport. She mindlessly followed the other children who were now walking out of the school in droves and headed in the direction of the Starehe Boys' Centre. She knew it wasn't too far off and some of the children lived in that area, so she did not have to walk alone. The large group of children split into two and Toni's group crossed the road at the junction, opposite Brilliant hotel. They then cut through Ngara estate and marched towards Kariokor then Ziwani, their young legs covering a lot of ground quickly. The area was not among the safest places in Nairobi, but they were just school children in uniform and only an insane person would dare harm them, they thought.

"What are you doing here?" Her father gasped, shocked to see her standing outside the staff room. He had just come out of a class and was surprised to see his daughter standing at the edge of the short staircase, barely two hours after he'd dropped her off at school.

"Our headmaster died last night. The school has been closed," she replied.

Her father opened the staff room door to usher her in. Two teachers sat at the end of a long table that ran the length of the room, marking papers.

"Sit here," her father ordered, patting one of the chairs.

"Hi Toni, are you unwell?" Mrs Njoroge asked, turning her attention to Toni. She was a fat, chubby teacher with a beautiful, round face. Toni liked her very much.

"Mr Mwangi, her headmaster, is no more," Toni's father announced to his colleagues. Those words again, Toni thought to herself. "No More". She replayed the words several times in her head and the thought that she would ever have to use the words again filled her with fear.

"Mr. Mwangi is no more," she replayed the words in her mind. The impact and consequences of death were foreign subjects to Toni. Nobody had ever died in her family. All she knew was that when people died, they went to heaven, like Jesus, as she had been taught in Sunday School.

Toni's parents had had it with living in the staff quarters of Starehe Boys'.

"It's about time we own our own house," her father had said. He took a loan from the bank and bought a two-bedroomed house in Ayany Estate. Ayany Estate was not what one would call a serene or posh neighbourhood, but it was neat, organised, and new. The houses had been built for the growing middle class of Nairobi. The roads were clean, and each house had its own garden. There were street lights and well-done roads, complete with ditches for drainage. Even though it was a new estate, Ayany Estate shared a border with one of Africa's largest slum dwellings, Kibera, which somewhat took the shine off its lustre. Kibera, like many slums, is renowned for its overcrowding, poverty, crime, disease, and lack of sanitation.

"But what about my friends?" Toni had complained, when she learnt that they would be moving to a new house.

"You'll make new ones, Toni. Don't worry. You make friends easily," her mother had consoled her.

Moving from Starehe to Ayany meant a longer journey from home to school, because the two were on opposite sides of Nairobi. Toni had been looking forward to walking home from school when she was a bit older, but that would no longer be possible.

Toni's first friend in Ayany was Antoinette. Their next-door neighbour, Bakari, was Antoinette's uncle. The two girls met one weekend when Antoinette had come to visit her uncle and aunt. Antoinette was of mixed race and had long, flowing straight hair and brown eyes. She was a bit taller than Toni even though she was a year younger. Toni and Antoinette both loved playing with dolls. They would go around the estate, begging tailors for bits of fabric, that they would use to make rag dolls and dresses for the dolls. But that wasn't all that made Toni and Antoinette very close. Antoinette's mum was from the Seychelles. Her whole family spoke French, which mesmerised Toni every time she visited her friend.

She loved the way Antoinette's uncles called her "Mamzelle" and the way they danced "Sega", their traditional dance, with their wives and girlfriends.

Toni practised the little French she learnt from Teacher Jacques, whenever she went to Antoinette's house. Antoinette also lived in Ayany Estate, but a few blocks away from Toni. The estate was organised in alphabetical order. Toni's house was in the K section while Antoinette lived in the M section. An entire section, L, separated them.

It took Toni ten minutes to get to Antoinette's home. To her dismay, Toni quickly realized that her trips across the estate to Antoinette's house wouldn't be as easy as she had initially thought.

All because of one Asaph, a stout, tough-looking, nine-year-old meanie who lived in L. He would kick Toni, pull her hair, try to sweep her off her feet and give her endless knocks on the head with his knuckles. She always tried to run past the area when Asaph was not looking, but often, he was outside playing, and he would run after her.

One evening, as Toni and Antoinette were bracing themselves for Asaph's bullying, they came across a strange sight. Asaph was on his knees, looking for something in the grass, tears rolling down his face. He looked so unhappy that the girls forgot he was a bully, for an instant.

"What is it Asaph?" Toni asked sweetly.

"I've lost my father's cigarettes; he's going to thrash me with his belt," he sobbed.

It turned out that Asaph's father had sent him to the "kiosk" for cigarettes, but he had lost them on his way home. A beating was definitely in store for the boy. The only discipline measure parents knew when Toni was growing up was caning. Most parents were ardent believers and faithful practitioners of the adage "spare the rod and spoil the child." They gladly turned to a belt or cane every time their children did something wrong.

Even though Asaph was a bully and made Toni's life hell, she sympathised with him because his father had the reputation of violence. It was said that he often hit Asaph's mother too! Toni could not imagine her father lifting a finger against her mum. He was strict with her and her brother, but he was gentle and loving to their mother.

Suddenly, Toni broke into laughter, pointing at Asaph. "You're so silly! The cigarettes are behind your ears!"

For a second, Asaph looked confused. He fumbled with his ears and pulled out the two cigarettes that he had tucked behind them, to free his hands for play, and most probably, to be able to pull Toni's hair. The small boy was so relieved, he grabbed Toni and hugged her tight.

He said, "I'll never bully you again, Toni. I'm so sorry. Thank you for finding my father's cigarettes."

After the incident with Asaph, life for Toni became more enjoyable in the estate. Asaph was a ring-leader and being his friend brought along a lot of new friends.

When Toni and Antoinette were not sewing dolls, they would join the other children to play outside. They would play *Shake, Kati, Blada*, and Hide and Seek until dinner time. *Kati* was a ball game, where two players tried to hit a third player, who was in the middle, with a ball. The ball was made using old plastic bags. *Blada*, Toni's favourite game, involved the use of an old rubber tube cut into a long strip that two girls held on either end, as a third girl tried to jump over it, without touching it. The height would be raised after each successful jump.

One evening, as Toni was playing with one of her dolls, Uncle Kimondo, who lived in Kiambu, came to visit. Kiambu, where Toni's father grew up, was about fifteen kilometres from Nairobi and was known for its lush tea plantations and beautiful green scenery. Unlike Nairobi with its noise and pollution, Kiambu had fresh and cool air. The population was made up mostly of farmers.

Toni's father had a tea farm in Kiambu, where he employed workers to pick tea and take to the factory. Uncle Kimondo worked in the farm as a supervisor; ensuring that the workers did not steal. Apart from his protruding stomach and unkempt hair, Uncle Kimondo had a huge appetite for food which reminded Toni of the ogre in "Jack and the Beanstalk," who could never eat enough.

Uncle Kimondo always showed up at mealtimes and would not leave until he had eaten at least two servings. As soon as the meal was served, he would attack his plate of food, looking around the table as he chewed noisily.

As usual, Uncle Kimondo said that he had a very important message for Toni's father from the village. As Toni's father hadn't come home yet; he would have to spend the night.

"Phanice, please take this money and run to the kiosk. Buy a packet of milk and a loaf of bread," Toni's mother instructed. Phanice had been peeling potatoes for dinner.

She put the knife down, wiped her hands, took the cash from her boss's hands, and headed for the door.

Uncle Kimondo looked up then quickly down, hiding a smile behind the newspaper he was pretending to read.

"Mum, please, can I go with Phanice? Pleeeeeeease!" Toni begged.

"Fine. Hurry up before it gets dark," her mother said. It was a bit late for afternoon tea but in Toni's house, a visitor was always welcomed with a cup of tea and bread. Unfortunately, all the bread at the kiosk had been sold out for the day. Uncle Kimondo had to settle for a cup of white tea only.

"I'm sorry, there was no bread at the kiosk. Please have this cup of tea as Phanice prepares dinner," Toni's mother offered in the way of an apology.

Uncle Kimondo neither forgave, nor forgot the incident. A few months later, when Toni and her family went to Kiambu to visit, Uncle Kimondo pulled Toni aside and whispered, "Toni, just tell me the truth. That day I came to your house, was it your mum who told you to say there was no bread at the kiosk, or was it true that there was really no bread?"

Toni replied, a little too loudly, "Why are you whispering? It was true! The kiosk had run out of bread. I'm going to tell my mum what you said."

Chapter FOUR

Antoinette's uncle, Bakari, had rented out his servants' quarters to Musa, a single, twenty-five-year-old man. Musa was a neat, soft-spoken man who worked as a messenger for an engineering company. Children in the estate loved Musa because he bought them sweets from the kiosk and played them his guitar when he wasn't working.

On Saturdays, they would gather around his small flat and chant Daudi Kabaka's famous song "Pole Musa," until Musa came out, pretending to storm out and try to run after the children, without ever really catching any of them. Toni and her friends would take off in various directions, shrieking in delight. They would repeat the song until Musa was too tired or too bored to continue.

One Saturday morning, with Toni leading the chants, the children came out to play. They sang the usual song, but Musa did not come out of his house. The troupe moved closer and kept up the song, but there was no response from Musa. There was no sound, not even the usual Reggae beats from Musa's guitar that always announced his presence.

Musa did not come out of his flat for a whole week, and when he eventually did, he had to be carried out of his house by the police who had had to break down his door when their knocks went unanswered.

Neighbours gathered around the house, murmuring, and shaking their heads sadly. The children, who had been closer to Musa than any of the adult neighbours, were shooed away and not allowed anywhere near the scene.

"Mummy, what happened to Musa?" Toni asked her mother who was standing next to her husband, along with the other neighbours.

"He was sick," was the only reply.

"Will he get better?" Toni insisted.

As the police carried Musa's body out in a body bag, Toni's father said, in a grave voice, "Toni, Musa is no more."

Musa had been found dead in his house, after his boss alerted the police, because he hadn't reported to work for a week, and nobody seemed to know where he was. Tears flowed down Toni's cheeks.

She now knew what the words "no more" meant. She turned to Antoinette and said, "We'll never see Musa again. He'll never play the guitar again. He's gone up to heaven like Mr Mwangi."

Two years after joining City Primary, Toni heard about the much acclaimed "Wildlife Club", which admitted the best-behaved pupils only after obtaining written permission from their parents. The members proudly wore a "Kenya Wildlife Service" badge on their sweaters or blazers. They also had a yearly trip to one of Kenya's game parks, which cost a lot of money.

The written permission would be handed to the patron of the club, Mr Mwagozi, who would either approve or disapprove. If he approved, the existing members of the club would then decide if they wanted the pupil to join the club.

"Daddy, I'm joining the Wildlife Club. But first you have to sign this paper so that I can take it to Mr Mwagozi tomorrow," Toni announced to her father one evening. Her father took the paper from her hands, and on reading it gasped aloud.

"Toni! We don't have this kind of money. I'm sorry," he said.

"It's okay," Toni began, "I don't have to go for the trips; I just want to have the badge."

Her father hesitantly scribbled his signature on the paper.

"Thank you, Daddy!" Toni responded delightedly. She would deal with the trips when the time came. Toni was accepted into the club and like all new members, was required to introduce herself before all members during the weekly meeting. She wore her newest school dress that morning. The meetings took place on Friday afternoons, which the school had set aside for club activities.

The Wildlife Club had a "board" with a chairperson, a secretary, and a treasurer. These three sat at the front of the class facing the other members, bathing in the glowing pride that came with holding such esteemed positions. Mr Mwagozi, the patron, sat on a chair in the corner, following the proceedings closely and only cut in if need arose. Francis, the chairman, and the brightest boy in the school, also happened to be the school head boy. Toni thought he was so handsome; she almost fainted when he introduced her as the newest member.

"Please welcome Toni, our latest member," he boomed as he held out one hand to welcome her. Toni felt nervous and could feel all the forty eyes of the old members on her back, as she walked to the front of the class.

"Toni, could you please tell us about yourself and why you chose to join our club?"

Toni looked at the club members, cleared her throat and launched into repeating what her friend Kate, who was already a member, had advised: "I joined this club because I love all animals and I'd like to protect them from poachers."

However, the truth was Toni did not like any animal – wild or domestic; if anything, she had a deep phobia for cats. Any time she saw a cat, even her mother's, she either poured water on it or threw stones at it to chase it away. She had joined the Wildlife Club because she wanted to be part of the posh children in school, and for the annual trips to game parks. Plus, all the dashing, clever boys belonged to the Wildlife Club.

Shortly after, Mr Mwagozi announced that the club would be visiting the Tsavo National Park.

"All the members are going. I'll be the only one who won't go. Surely, you can't let your child be the only one in the whole club who's not going," Toni whined to her parents when she got home.

"You never give up, do you Toni? I thought we had this discussion before you joined the club," her father replied, shaking his head as if in disbelief.

"How will I feel when everybody is discussing the trip? How would you feel if it were you?" Toni pleaded.

Tsavo, one of the oldest national parks in the country, is split into east and west by a railway line. It is located near Voi town, on the way to the Indian Ocean.

A Kenya Wildlife Service bus transported the excited children to the park. They would spend four days and three nights away. The journey from Nairobi to Tsavo takes about five hours by road, but it took longer because they stopped at Mtito Andei for a picnic, and because the road was bumpy and had many potholes. When they got to Tsavo, they pitched their tents on the campsite. Toni shared a tent with her friend Kate.

Very early the next morning, they set off by bus for a game drive. Tsavo has a lot of elephants and giraffes. Toni had never seen an elephant before; she was shocked at how big it was. The children saw a lot of animals, except lions which prefer the savannah.

After the game drive, they went back to the tented camp for dinner. There were a lot of white tourists, having dinner or relaxing by the poolside. The children then gathered around a huge bonfire. A guest from the Kenya Wildlife Service had come to give a talk, educating them on why poaching was bad for the country.

"Excuse me, sir, what is an endangered species?" Toni asked.

The guest speaker looked around and asked if any of the other children knew the meaning of the words. All the children shook their heads.

"Well, well, well... Thank you, young lady, for being bold enough to ask a question that nobody had the answer to. An endangered species is an animal that is facing danger from bad human beings, like poachers, for example," the guest speaker said.

Shortly after the guest speaker left, Mr Mwagozi told the children that they had an hour before bedtime, but they could do something interesting in that time.

As if on cue, the children started singing songs that Toni did not know. Whitney Houston's smashing hit song, *"How Will I Know"* was a favourite among the girls, so was Madonna's *"Papa Don't Preach,"* Michael Jackson's *"Thriller"* and countless other songs by Stevie Wonder.

The group of young Wildlife Club members sang the songs word for word as if they had written the lyrics themselves or had already fallen in and out of love a few times. Toni felt uncomfortable and wondered where and how the other children had learnt the songs. Toni's family only had a small radio cassette player at home, that her father kept in his bedroom. She had heard some of the songs on the radio in the car, on their way to school, but she had never thought about them. That was going to change.

As soon as she arrived back home after the trip, Toni got a fresh exercise book from the pile her father kept in a bookshelf. She labelled it "My Songs". Every time she heard one of the songs from the trip, she jotted down the words, until she had all the lyrics.

"Toni don't tell me you're finishing your homework in the car again. How many times have I...." her father began, looking at the rear-view mirror, as he drove his children to school, one morning.

"Daddy, she's not doing her homework, she's writing down songs," Ken interrupted, before Toni could say anything.

"And Ken is drawing cartoons," Toni also reported.

"Ken, if your teacher tells me you've been drawing under the desk instead of working in class, I'll give you a double beating," their father warned. Toni stuck her tongue out at her brother, and Ken did the same at her. Ken was not interested in maths or history, or any other subject except for fine art. He was the best in his class and always said he was going to be an artist when he grew up.

"That is not a serious career," Toni's father would tell Ken, who didn't seem to hear.

In her last year of primary school, she joined the club on a tour of the Masai Mara Game Reserve, which is famed for the wondrous wildebeest migration and its large population of lions. The lions awed Toni.

"One look at you and you get goosebumps," she told Ken when she got back.

This time around, Toni knew all the latest songs, word for word. She had crammed even the beats of the music. At the bonfire, the boys looked at her in admiration and some of the girls felt a twinge of jealousy.

The Maasai Mara Game Reserve
Photo by Mick Flynn

In October, during her last year in primary school, with Kenya Certificate of Primary Education exams around the corner, Toni had a lot of revision to do if she wanted to make it to a good high school, a school which taught French. Every morning, her father would wake her up at 4.00am, with a gentle shake, whispering, "Toni, Toni, it's time to get up."

Toni shared a bedroom with Ken and Phanice. There were two double-decker beds crammed into the small bedroom. She slept on the top bed of the first decker while Phanice slept on the lower bed. Ken slept on the top bed of the other decker. The bottom bed was for female visitors. Any male visitor who had to spend the night would sleep on one of the sofas in the living room.

After waking his daughter up, Toni's father would go back to bed, leaving Toni alone in the living room, studying at the dining table. Her mother, Ken and Phanice were all deep asleep. At six o'clock, Toni would put her books in her school bag and go to their bedroom to change from her nightdress to her school uniform.

Ken would already be awake and dressed in his Starehe Boys' uniform. After breakfast, the whole family got into their white Toyota corolla and left for the day. Toni's father dropped his wife off in the city centre then proceeded to City Primary to drop Toni, before heading to Starehe.

One Sunday, a cousin called Wahome came to visit. He had a habit of turning up unexpected and putting up for days before moving on to another relative.

"I've found a *kibarua* (a casual job) at a hotel in town," Wahome said. "I hope you don't mind if I stay for a few days as I look for my own place," he added.

Wahome had to sleep in the living room because Toni's parents would never allow a man to share a bedroom with their children and the househelp. This created problems for the family: First, this complicated Toni's study routine in the morning and inconvenienced her parents because they liked watching TV after the children had gone to bed. Secondly, and worse so, Wahome had smelly feet, no matter the time of day. Even right after taking a bath, his feet still let out a horrible, nauseating stench that would fill the room within minutes and drive everybody out. Dinnertime became torture, as one had to hold their breath the entire time while chewing their food.

As soon as they finished dinner, Toni and Ken would disappear into their bedroom, and Toni's parents would claim to be tired and go to bed early. Wahome would then be left alone in the living room, switching between channels on the TV, his smelly feet up on the sofa.

Days turned into weeks and still Wahome showed no signs of leaving. One evening, when Wahome had traveled upcountry to visit his parents, Toni's father turned to her, "Toni, you have to tell him. This cannot go on anymore. He has to leave."

"Why can't you tell him Daddy?" Toni protested. "He's your nephew."

"But that's precisely why I can't tell him," her father countered.

"I don't want him to go running his mouth in the village that I chased him away from my home."

"Then why can't Ken tell him?" Toni protested.

"Toni, you 're the only one with the guts to tell him," replied Ken.

When Wahome came back from work, Toni waited until everybody was asleep and he was, as usual, flipping through the channels. He had settled on "*Usiniharakishe*" – Kiswahili for "don't rush me" – a controversial show the government was intent on banning for it showed kissing scenes.

"Wahome," Toni began, throwing a quick look at his feet, and sitting as far away from him as she could. "I have something to ask you."

Wahome sat up, lowered the volume of the TV, and turned his head towards her attentively. He was a handsome young man with a lovely, cunning smile.

"Yes, Toni?" He responded, with one raised eyebrow.

"Have you found your flat?" Toni continued. The question caught Wahome off-guard.

"Yes, I have," Wahome lied, glancing about the room, avoiding her eyes. "In fact, I'm planning to move out next week," he said, clearly shocked by the question.

"Which day exactly, please?" Toni prodded.

"Errrrmm, on Tuesday..." Wahome said hesitantly.

The next morning, at breakfast, Toni announced to the whole family, "Wahome is moving out on Tuesday next week.

"Phanice, can you make *chapatis*, exceptionally, for Monday dinner? Just to say thanks to Wahome and to say bye because we might not see him for a long time."

Toni's strategy worked. On Tuesday morning, Wahome packed his few clothes into his old bag and bid the family goodbye. He had found another relative to hang on to for a few weeks.

On Sundays, Toni and her family attended the Nairobi Baptist Church. Her parents went for the main adult service, while Toni and Ken joined the other teenagers for the youth fellowship. Toni enjoyed the singing and worship in church, but sometimes found the sermons a bit too long. After church they would either go back home or visit her Aunt Susan or other friends. Toni hated going back home because her father always had chores for her and her brother.

This was one of those Sundays when they went back home. Phanice, as was the case every Sunday, was away for it was her off day, so Toni and Ken carried out her duties.

"Toni! Ken! When you finish your food and wash the dishes, you will clean the car. Outside and inside. Remove all the mats and scrub them. After that you will each do a maths exercise then give me your book review for this week," Toni's father ordered.

He obliged them to read a book per week and write a review that he corrected.

"Reading is very important. You learn a lot of new things, you build your vocabulary and you learn how to express yourself correctly," he would repeat often.

Toni grumbled about her life with her parents as she dragged her feet to the kitchen. Why couldn't her father leave her alone?

Antoinette never had to clean her father's car or read a book every week. She secretly envied Antoinette, whose family was so much fun.

"My father is so strict. I wish he went out to bars in the evenings, like the other fathers," Toni usually confided in Antoinette.

"He's always at home, dishing out chores like an army commander, making my life hell. It's all about studying and cleaning in our house," she would add.

As she was drying off the last plate, Toni had a brainwave. She knew she would pay dearly for it, but the urge was stronger than the cost that would follow. Pretending to wipe the table, she confirmed that her parents were napping on the sofa, as they did every Sunday after lunch. She tiptoed out of the house. Ken had already started cleaning the car. He dipped his rag into the bucket of soapy water and rubbed the dirt off the side of the car. Toni passed him and went to the gate, opening it slowly to avoid making any noise.

"Where are you going?" Ken asked.

"It's none of your business," Toni retorted as she closed the gate and took off, running, in the direction of Antoinette's house.

Antoinette's mother opened the gate when Toni rang the bell. Toni admired Antoinette's mum because she spoke French and wore make-up all the time.

"Hey Toni, come on in! Antoinette and her cousins are at the back of the house."

Toni joined the teenagers, who were playing cards around a garden table. Ronny, Antoinette's cousin, was easily the most handsome boy Toni had ever seen. He was in high school and, in Toni's mind, so cool that she kept stealing glances at him.

The afternoon was great, watching Antoinette's uncles dancing Sega with their wives or girlfriends. There was a lot of beer and some of the adults smoked – even the women – much to Toni's surprise.

"Toni, your brother is here," announced Antoinette's mum, who had come out of the house, holding a glass of wine in one hand, and a cigarette in the other.

"Oh no," sighed Antoinette. Why had Ken come?

A smiling Ken appeared and said loudly, "Toni! Daddy says you should go back home immediately! You didn't ask for permission to come here and he's going to beat you!"

That evening, when Toni got back home, her father gave her several strokes of his wide belt, for having left the house without saying.

"Why don't you just kill me?" Toni screamed at her father as the belt landed on her hands and legs. "Or take me back to my real parents! Why did you adopt me in the first place, if you hate me this much?" She went on.

Toni's rudeness infuriated her father even more, driving him to raise the belt even higher and bring it down with more force, so much so that by the time he was done with her, Toni's hands were swollen from all the beating. Toni's mother had to put herself between her husband and her daughter to stop the beatings.

Despite her striking resemblance to her mother, Toni sometimes liked to imagine that her parents had adopted her from an orphanage, and that was why they were so strict – or as she loved to tell Antoinette, mean – with her.

Chapter FIVE

Secondary schools in Kenya were divided into three categories: national schools, which only admitted top students who'd scored the highest marks in the KCPE (Kenya Certificate of Primary Education) exams; provincial schools, which took the students who had narrowly missed qualifying for the national schools; and district schools, which admitted the rest of the students.

Toni had been a good pupil, always among the top ten in her primary school. But a national school was a bit out of her league and she knew it. In any case, Toni didn't care; if the school taught French, she was happy to go there. The pupils had to choose five schools of their choice: one national, two provincial and two district schools.

"Choose Limuru Girls as your national school, Toni," advised her mother. "You can go visiting Aunt Jane when you're on break."

"Never!" replied Toni, a bit too loudly. "I hate their uniform and Limuru is way too cold."

"Limuru is just next to Kiambu; it's not any colder," her father replied, from the sofa where he was reading a newspaper. There was no way Toni was going to choose Limuru Girls, she insisted. She opted for Kenya High School, which was in Nairobi.

After sitting the KCPE exam, the pupils had to wait for over two months, before they could know their results and the secondary schools they had been admitted to. Those two months were days of sweet relief for Toni: no homework, no revision, and no book reviews. For the first time in her life, her father left her alone, most of the time.

"Toni, I have a letter for you," her father said one evening, handing her a white envelope.

"Hooray! I've been called to Moi Nairobi Girls!" Toni exclaimed, after reading the letter. She had chosen Moi Nairobi Girls, a prestigious all-girls boarding school, as her first provincial school, because they taught French and it was not far from Ayany Estate. "Kabbz" was the school's nickname, derived from the cabbage garden that ensured the girls had a balanced meal every day.

Toni was convinced that she was a disobedient girl, because of her father's beatings. But the cheekiness she observed at her high school made her feel like a small child. At Kabbz, Form 2 students were the naughtiest, and many of them were punished daily.

Take Wambui, a notorious dare-devil, for example. She had shortened her skirt and made it so tight that her buttocks stuck out and her hips bulged from the sides. Mrs Macharia, the headmistress, had once described her as a "bursting sausage" because she could hardly walk in the tight skirt. Tanya, who spoke in a raucous, grating voice, would wear her tie so long that it protruded from her sweater and went all the way to her knees. Lucy had chopped off the sleeves of her blouse and walked around with a swagger. One mean word and she looked like she would pull out a gun from her holster and kill you in cold blood.

The weekly inspection at assembly always promised sufficient action and laughter, which did not amuse the teachers at all. The offenders would, in addition to other forms of punishment, spend hours kneeling in front of the staffroom or digging in the school garden.

Toni marvelled at the girls' courage – or was it stupidity? She never could put her finger on it. She would never dare do some of the things the girls did, like copying the next student's work or answers during exams. Her father would surely kill her, she thought.

However, an incident between Toni and her father would stay with her for life. It was opening day, the evening that she returned to school after a long holiday. They had a holiday once every three months. Parents could visit their daughters on a set Sunday, once a month. Her father had driven her back to school. It was raining heavily.

"Here's your pocket money," he said, as he handed her a twenty shilling note.

Toni was seething with rage inside. She didn't understand why he gave her such little pocket money. Some girls came from more modest backgrounds, but their parents still managed to give them at least a hundred shillings. Sometimes her mother sneaked her a fifty-shilling note when her father wasn't looking and made her promise not to tell him. But on that day, her mum had been at work, and had forgotten to give her extra cash. She would have only twenty shillings for the three months.

"I'm fed up with your twenty shillings! You can keep it," she snapped at her father, who was so surprised at her outburst that he didn't react immediately.

Ten minutes later, as Toni stood in the rain with her suitcase half open from the force with which her father had thrown it out of the trunk, and her belongings getting soaked, she cried in anger and wondered why her father was so hard on her. She did her best, she had never been suspended from school, or been caught drinking alcohol in the dormitory. To Toni, her father treated her as if she were the worst child a parent could have.

Mr Mutiso, Toni's English teacher, was a soft-spoken man of medium height. He usually wore a green or brown suit and all sorts of coloured shirts but never once missed a tie. His style was old-fashioned but elegant and seemed to lift his spirits. The trousers were flared and the shoes a bit higher than what was trending in the nineties. He was the most eloquent person Toni had ever heard speak. He had a clean, nasal British accent and taught the girls how to pronounce words correctly. He was blind and walked with a white stick that he tapped the ground with, to avoid obstacles.

One day Tanya, who sat in a corner at the back of the class, bought sliced bread from the school tuck shop and started eating it in Mr Mutiso's class.

"Tanya, can you get out of my class immediately! You're up for punishment for eating bread in class!" Mr Mutiso suddenly shouted. Tanya froze and all the girls who had been smiling opened their eyes wide in shock. The naughty girls who had initially thought they could get away with all sorts of mischief, quickly realized that what Mr Mutiso did not have in sight, he had in double razor-sharp senses; not only could he smell the bread but could also know exactly which girl was eating it and perhaps, Toni thought, even tell the brand. Mr Mutiso had a list of all the class members in braille, including the sitting arrangement and would, on picking up a scent, stop in the middle of a lesson and call out one of the mischievous girls. His punishment was also the worst, according to all the students. His favourite one was making an offender write down a thousand lines saying, "I will never eat in class again." Mr Mutiso's sense of hearing was equally remarkable and would pick up even the faintest of murmurs. When a girl tried to read a novel under the desk, he would hear the ruffling of the pages right from the front of the class and another punishment would be meted out on the spot.

Toni had looked forward to joining high school for one reason: She could finally learn French properly and start speaking it. She was looking forward to learning the rules of grammar, writing long sentences, and reading thick novels in French. But, to her disappointment, her teachers of French in Moi Nairobi Girls turned out to be very different from Teacher Jacques. While he was a French native, her teachers were all Kenyan and spoke French with an accent that didn't sound like French to Toni. They sounded like they were speaking an African dialect that she was not familiar with. The lessons were boring, and theoretical at best. The teachers never gave the girls a chance to practise speaking, and anyway, the teachers themselves spoke more English than French.

As much as she loved the language, her motivation dropped to near zero and each term she struggled to get good grades. She however, enjoyed the Wildlife Club, which she had enrolled in as soon as she joined Moi Nairobi Girls. Apart from the usual safaris, camping trips and visits to the museum, the high school chapter also held debates with wildlife clubs from boys' schools. Toni had turned out to be quite a good debater and often made part of the team that represented her club. It is during one of those debates in her third year of high school that she stumbled upon John Mark, who was representing his school in a debate. He was a slim young man with a light complexion, and black-rimmed glasses. John Mark went to Lenana school, one of the prestigious boys' national schools in Nairobi.

He had bounced up to the podium, gently pushed his glasses up his nose, cleared his throat, then begun in a velvety voice, "Thank you Mr. Chairman," with a slight nod of his head. "Honourable judges, adjudicators, teachers, and my fellow students," he had said, opening out his hands as if he was spreading confetti to the guests at a wedding.

"I stand here before you this afternoon to strongly oppose this motion that says, 'Boarding schools should be abolished'. But, before I move on to my points, I would like to humbly refute a few points brought forth by one of my worthy opponents..."

And then he had turned to look at Toni. She had spoken just before him, so she was the worthy opponent he was referring to. It was important for Toni to listen to him and note down his remarks, to counter his argument when she came back to conclude. But the minute her eyes met with John Mark's, her heart missed a beat and she went deaf. She couldn't hear what he was saying. She couldn't stop staring at him, at the way he moved his body when he spoke.

She felt like she was in a tunnel and there was water gushing past her, drowning out any other noise. Toni didn't realize it then, but she had just fallen hopelessly in love for the first time in her life. She was sixteen and he was seventeen.

For two years after that, Toni constantly thought about John Mark, replaying images of him in her head. She longed to see him, but she didn't know how to go about it. Their schools didn't meet for any more debates. She started writing him letters during prep time in the evenings.

"I think about you all the time John Mark, and I hope we shall meet again."

Sometimes it was a short poem or quote: "If only wishes were flowers, I'd pick the loveliest and send them to you" or the lyrics of a song: "And I will always love you." Letters that she never sent because she was too timid and unsure.

She stored the letters in a shoe box that she hid in her locker, behind her clothes. As the months flew by, the shoe box filled with letters and poems and cut-out love hearts.

One day during the holidays, she bumped into John Mark at a church function, where youth from other churches had been invited. By then he'd already finished high school and was waiting for his Kenya Certificate of Secondary Education (KCSE) exams results. Before they parted, he told her what he was doing with himself.

"I work at my aunt's bookshop in town. You can pass by to see me if you want. It's on Kimathi Street; between Uchumi Supermarket and the shoe shop," he told her.

In the subsequent weeks, Toni would make numerous visits to the shop just to see John Mark and talk to him. Every visit would last only five minutes, but it took her a whole hour to make a trip to and from the shop.

John Mark was friendly and polite, but never once proposed a movie, or an outing together. Clearly, he was not interested in her. She stopped going to the shop and tried to forget him.

A year later, when Toni joined the university, John Mark strolled back into her life. It was on a sunny afternoon, on her way back from the Alliance Française library, where she spent a lot of her time. It was a nice surprise. He was still as handsome as the last time she had seen him.

"Hey, would you like to meet up sometime next week?" John Mark quipped as soon as they had exchanged pleasantries. He was in the company of two girls and seemed to be in a hurry.

"Are you sure?" Toni returned, looking over his shoulders at the two girls.

"Yes, I am sure. Friday 4pm at Wimpy. Okay?" He said cheerfully before his face cracked into a warm smile.

"Fine," Toni nodded. "See you then. I think your friends are waiting for you," she added with a mischievous smile.

John Mark was already at Wimpy when Toni got

there, but with company: A girl with whom he was chatting excitedly.

"Hello Toni, meet my cousin Maureen. I just ran into her here, waiting for her friend who is running late. So, I asked her to sit here with me as she waits."

"Hi Maureen," Toni was relieved to learn that Maureen was John Mark's cousin and nothing more. "How are your classes?" He asked, pointing at the bag Toni was carrying. It was a neat and colourful leather pouch that Aunt Susan had brought her from her last trip to France. It was small enough to carry around easily and big enough to fit a few text books.

"Great, but this is something I brought for you", she said, with a naughty smile and a twinkle in her eye.

"Really?" John Mark asked in genuine surprise, wondering what Toni could possibly be carrying.

"Yes, but later," Toni dismissed him before beckoning to a waiter.

"Masala tea and a sausage please," she said before carefully placing the bag on an empty seat. Toni felt awkward, not knowing what to talk about with John Mark and his cousin. Thankfully, Maureen took off as soon as her friend arrived.

"So," Toni began casually, reaching out for the bag. "I've been meaning to give these to you. Since they are yours, you might as well have them," she said, revealing the contents of the bag.

John Mark opened his mouth wide, as dozens of letters spilled out of the bag onto the table.

"What are these? Mine? All of them?" He said, openly awed.

"Yeah... All yours," Toni replied, smiling at him cheekily and feeling proud of herself. "I've always been interested in you, er, romantically, but since I didn't have the guts to tell you, I resorted to writing you letters."

"And just kept them?" John Mark gasped.

"Listen, I didn't know what to do. Now, take them, read them or throw them away," Toni said in a tone that suggested a change of topic.

"I have also been interested in you," John Mark began, looking at Toni straight in the eye, making her heart melt, all over again. "I didn't think you liked me, that's why I never said anything."

Toni rolled her eyes and suddenly felt shy and uncomfortable. "Look, I have to go. My curfew is 6.00pm. If I'm not home by then my old man will kill me."

"I'll walk you to your bus stop," John Mark offered.

They had barely walked two hundred meters when John Mark put his arm around her shoulder and gently turned her towards a deserted back alley.

"Where are we going?" Toni protested.

His wordless response came swiftly and in the most unexpected of ways. He stood in front of her, her back leaning against a wall, lowered his head, pressed his lips against hers and began to kiss her gently, running his tongue along the inner part of her lips. His lips felt so soft and warm. She didn't resist it and kissed him back, the way she saw couples kiss on TV. John Mark reached down under her skirt and caressed her thigh, sending an electric sensation through her body. His hand was moving up her thigh, flirting with her panty. As one finger pushed into her panty, realisation of where she was and what she was doing hit her like a slap.

"Stop!" She begged, suddenly switching to panic mode. What if one of her parents' friends passed by and saw her? She thought and panicked even some more.

She was a good Christian girl. Only bad girls did this kind of thing. What would her parents think? She pried herself loose and took off towards her bus-stop. She ran all the way to the famous Kencom stage to catch her bus home.

Her heart was beating fast and it wasn't only from the running. John Mark's kiss had caught her totally by surprise. She could hardly think. It took her a few minutes to calm down. She looked at her watch. Damn, it was almost six o'clock. She hoped the bus wouldn't take too long and that Ngong road wouldn't have its usual crazy traffic, especially around the City Mortuary. Better still, she hoped her father wouldn't be home.

Then she noticed a familiar figure walking towards the bus stop, tapping away at the road and at the sides with a white stick. He was in a green suit and a red tie. He stopped a few metres away from her.

"Hello. Could you please tell me when the number twenty comes?" He said to a man standing nearby. The unmistakable British accent pulled Toni closer to him.

Toni walked up to him and touched his left arm.

"Hello Mr Mutiso," Toni said, making him turn towards the direction of her voice. His lips broke into a smile.

"Hello young lady. I recognise your voice. You are Toni from the 1989 form two class, aren't you?" He said, more like a statement than a question. "What are you up to these days?"

Toni was impressed by his sharp memory. She almost replied, "If you only knew...", as she remembered John Mark's lips against hers and his hand up her skirt.

In her late teens, Toni got "born again". According to the Protestant faith, when one accepted Jesus into their life, Jesus became a personal saviour and the person was said to be "born again" or "saved".

During her school holidays, Toni religiously attended youth fellowships at the Nairobi Baptist Church and signed up for the Word of Life Christian camps, where speakers spoke to the teenagers about living a holy life before God.

As a "savedie," Toni stuck to her faith and avoided all sins, like listening to secular music, kissing boys, sex outside of marriage and anything that was unpleasant in the Lord's eyes. Her parents were happy that Toni was a good girl and didn't hang out with the wrong company. Antoinette and her family had by then moved out of Ayany Estate.

One day, Toni heard of this awesome new church which every young "savedie" in Nairobi was attending. It was called the Lighthouse Church, but everybody called it "Lighty". Lighty initially held its services at the posh Silver Springs Hotel in Hurlingham, but later moved to the City Stadium when the members became too many for the hotel conference room. The pastor, who was American, played a rock guitar, as the members danced and clapped as if they were in a nightclub. Toni loved it from the first day she attended. She stopped attending the Baptist church and became a staunch member of Lighty. Soon enough she was going to church up to three times every Sunday: for the morning service, evening service and for a Bible course in between the two services.

At the end of the Bible course, the pastor would baptise her by immersion. "But you're already baptised!", protested her parents, who were not too thrilled by this new "evangelical church" that their daughter had joined and which they thought was a cult.

Toni had begun referring to their church as "DCR (Dead Cold Religion)". She'd informed her parents that the joke of a baptism they had given her as a baby was not good enough. She wanted to be "immersed in water completely," the way John the Baptist had baptised Jesus. Toni also began to speak in tongues and to bind the devil loudly in her prayers.

"God is not deaf you know," her mother would tell her, in exasperation.

Members of Lighty were quite similar; at least in appearance. The men wore ties and suits and spoke with a nasal American accent like the senior pastor. They were perfect gentlemen, holding doors for the ladies, paying bills when they all went out for lunch. The ladies dressed decently; their skirts covered their knees, they did not show any cleavage and they did not wear too much make-up.

They were polite and a bit shy. Toni tried her best to emulate their behaviour, which sometimes wasn't easy, because naturally, she was far from being shy. The members also addressed each other as "Brother" and "Sister".

In Toni's eyes, Lighty members were the perfect Christians and she often wondered how they managed to be so holy so easily. She struggled not to lie, not to get angry when somebody hurt her. It seemed to come naturally to the others, but not to her.

Four years after Toni had joined Lighty, when she was in her last year at university, a terrible scandal erupted in the church. One of the most prominent brothers and fire-spitting prayer warriors had impregnated one of the sisters. Toni was horrified to learn that a lot of the members were not "walking the walk" and were sleeping with each other and drinking alcohol when they were not speaking in tongues and binding the devil at church.

Toni's Christian world crumbled and her faith in God and the teachings of the Bible was shaken to the core. It was like an innocent child discovering that the parents she had looked up to were in fact, criminals. She didn't know where to turn.

She decided to go back to the church she had referred to as "Dead Cold Religion," where, instead of the pastor playing a rock guitar and jumping up and down to "*What a Mighty God We Serve*," there was an old piano and songs like "*Nearer My God to Thee*" that were so slow and boring that Toni struggled to keep her eyes open. Getting up on a Sunday to take the bus to church became a difficult task.

Toni stopped speaking in tongues and constantly reading her Bible. Her brother Ken, who had never left the Baptist church, found her listening to a Whitney Houston cassette and chuckled, "Ha! Ha! Ha! I thought that was the Devil's music? What happened?"

After passing her Kenya Certificate of Secondary Education (KCSE), Toni was admitted to Kenyatta University, in Nairobi, to pursue a bachelor's degree in education, with French as her major. Kenyatta University (KU) is the second oldest public university in Kenya. It sits on a thousand acres of flat land off the Nairobi – Thika highway. It was divided into three zones: The Western zone, the Eastern zone and The Nyayo zone. Toni and Alison, her classmate, had a room in the Ruwenzori hostel, which was situated in the Western zone of the campus, almost a kilometre away from the main entrance. The lecture halls were spread out over the whole campus.

To Toni's wonderful surprise, the lecturers at KU all spoke fluent French and taught exclusively in French, firing up her excitement with the language all over again.

Miss Elizabeth, her grammar teacher, was a particular well of inspiration. She was young, beautiful, and full of life. Her accent was perfect, and Toni watched and hung onto her every word. Miss Elizabeth had studied in Brittany, France.

She was everything Toni longed to be: perfectly fluent in French, with a sassy sense of style. Sometimes Miss Elizabeth wore shorts and bright red lipstick and Toni often wondered how old she was, or whether she had a boyfriend. She was friendly and easygoing when you met her in the corridors, but she was strict and unforgiving in class. Toni decided that the minute she cleared her undergraduate studies, she was taking off for France, come hell or high water.

There was also Dr Barasa, the French linguistics teacher. From his appearance, Dr Barasa seemed stuck in the eighties. He always had on a pair of flared trousers, and in all sorts of crazy colours: light green, sky blue, and screaming yellow. He sported a long, neatly combed afro. To Toni, he looked like one of the Jackson Five members, albeit a bit older.

Toni loved listening to Dr Barasa, even though her grades in linguistics were nothing to write home about. She didn't like studying and sometimes wondered if it were possible to receive French intravenously. All she wanted was to speak fluent French for heaven's sake!

One afternoon, Toni and Alison were walking from Ruwenzori to one of their lectures, when they bumped into Andy, a third-year student whom Alison had met the week before at a Bible Study meeting. He was walking towards them, wearing an orange and white striped t-shirt and blue jeans.

"Hi ladies!" Andy said brightly, showing a row of super white teeth. He had a charming smile and spoke with a slight lisp.

"Ali, who is that guy? How old is he? What course is he taking?" Toni pelted her friend with all sorts of questions about Andy.

Alison said that she'd only met him once, but she would find out more at the next Bible Study. Or better still, why didn't Toni join her Bible Study group? But to Toni's disappointment, Andy wasn't at the Bible Study meeting the week that followed. It would be a few weeks before Toni would bump into him again.

Andy was hanging out at the Student Centre one afternoon, when Toni and Alison went there for lunch. He waved at them from far but didn't go over to their table to greet them. He seemed to be engrossed in a deep conversation with the girl who was sitting opposite him. The girl was tall and light-skinned. She had a big bust that was overflowing from her top, and big, round eyes. She was sipping Fanta from a straw, and Andy was drinking a Sprite.

Toni kept stealing glances at him, not really listening to what Alison was telling her, wishing she could get a chance to talk to him. Two weeks after, Andy came to Bible Study. To Toni's delight, he chose the chair next to her! For the one hour that the study lasted, she couldn't concentrate and had trouble turning the pages of her Bible and locating the verses she was supposed to be reading from. He had a very nice smelling perfume on, which Toni learnt was called 'Azzaro' and very expensive.

"Can I walk you to your hostel, Toni?" Andy asked her at the end of the session.

She was surprised he remembered her name. It was common for boys to escort girls back to their hostels at night, but Toni was elated that Andy had chosen her and not another "sister". As they walked through the "Cassandra crossing", a long path that led from the Eastern zone to the Western zone, Andy asked Toni a lot of questions about herself. They sat on a bench outside Ruwenzori hostel.

It was a warm evening and all the windows in the hostels were open to cool the rooms before nightfall. Some students cooked in their hostels on bare-wired cookers, because eating at the student's mess was too costly for them. The smell of *ugali* filled the air as the wind blew.

"Lucky Dube" and "Bob Marley" music was blasting from the male hostels, while the girls preferred to listen to "Kenny G" and "Maria Carey". There were also small groups of students walking back from the nearby slum, known as "KM" because it was a kilometer away from the campus. They had just fed on huge *chapatis* and watery stew from the ladies who sold food in the open-air kiosks. Some boys had taken some illicit liquor there and were staggering back to their hostels, calling out to the girls, "Hey Sweetie, come to my room; I have something nice for you."

Andy and Toni sat on the bench for hours, chatting, getting to know each other. He was a Bio-Chemistry major and was in his final undergraduate year. He was the first born of three children and the only male.

Before he left, he pecked her on the cheek and said, "Please come and see me in Menengai hostel whenever you want." He gave her his room number and repeated "Any day in the evening, after 6.00pm is okay." Toni was so excited; she could hardly sleep that night. He liked her! The week that followed was a bit complicated for her; she kept thinking about Andy and couldn't concentrate on her books. She had decided to wait a whole week before venturing to his room.

She didn't want him to think she was in love with him; good Christian girls didn't flirt with boys. But he was so handsome and smelt so heavenly that it was hard for Toni to ignore the feelings that thoughts about him stirred in her.

One week had gone by and Toni was ready to visit Andy. It was a twenty-minute walk from Ruwenzori to Menengai, which was in the Eastern zone, and she prayed he would be in his room. She had had no means to warn him, as there were no phones in the rooms, and she hadn't bumped into him anywhere on the campus. But he had said she could visit any evening, so she supposed he stayed in his room. She had chosen her little blue dress that everybody said looked good on her. She hoped Andy would think the same. She wore a little make-up. "A God-fearing girl should not look like a painting," the pastor had said during the sermon on Sunday. She did not want Andy to think she was in any way trying to seduce him.

His room was at the end of a long corridor and as she walked towards it, Toni felt nervous. She rarely went into hostels occupied by male students and the stories she had heard about them were a bit scary.

She almost turned back when a man who was walking towards her in the company of another man whistled and said, "Hey sexy, where are you going?"

The corridor was dimly lit and there was a strong, suffocating smell of body odour.

As she walked past one of the rooms, she heard a girl's voice say, "You're killing me... I'm dying..." Toni wondered whether she should go in and save the poor girl from whoever was hurting her. Then she heard a male voice say, "But you like it, don't you?" The girl replied, "Yes, I like it very much." Toni walked as fast as she could to Andy's room.

She knocked lightly on the door, but there was no response the first time. She rapped harder and this time she heard his voice but couldn't make out what he had said.

As Toni was wondering whether she should just turn back and leave, Andy opened the door and stuck his head out.

"Oh, hi Toni ...", his face looked strange, as if he had just woken up. He seemed to hesitate, then opened the door a bit wider. "Come in."

The room was like all the other rooms in the hostels: a bunker bed was fixed to one wall and there was a counter beneath the window sill. Across from the bed, on the opposite wall was a built-in closet that had space for a few clothes and shoes.

Andy wasn't alone in his room: there was a girl in bed, covering herself with the bed sheet, but one of her breasts was partially visible. Andy himself had only a towel wrapped around his waist. Toni recognised the girl; it was the same girl she had seen Andy talking to at the Student Centre.

Toni was confused. Wasn't Andy a Christian? He came for Bible Study, so he was. What was going on? She wished the ground would open right then and swallow her whole.

"I'm sorry," she stammered, as she walked back to the door and ran out of the room.

"Toni, wait!" She heard Andy start. But Toni was already halfway down the corridor and on her way to Ruwenzori, tears stinging her eyes.

Chapter SIX

In her third year of university; Toni went to see Dr Barasa, her linguistics lecturer.

"Dr Barasa, which town would you recommend in France? I'm thinking of flying out after graduation."

"Well," Dr Barasa said thoughtfully, tugging at his goatee with one hand and adjusting his glasses with the other as he spoke.

"I did all my eight years of studying in Toulouse, so I can only tell you about Toulouse. It's in the South West, about three hours from Spain by car. The winters aren't very harsh and it's a student town, so you get to make a lot of friends from all over the world."

Toni listened attentively and made a mental note to visit the French Cultural Centre at the earliest opportunity. At the French Cultural Centre, Toni gleaned more information about Toulouse, including how to apply to a university in France. She found out that she would have to sit a language exam first, which would then determine her eligibility. She fished around for more information about the entrance exam and discovered that it was no walk in the park. In fact, from what she learnt, there were more failure stories than success stories. Even teachers of French would often flunk the entry exam.

Toni decided she was going to take a chance; she had nothing to lose, after all. There were two parts to the exam: a written paper and a listening comprehension. The cassette had not been clear, and Toni hadn't understood much. She forgot about the exam the minute she walked out of the room, convinced she had failed.

The Bachelor of Education course was programmed to take four years, and it did, but most of that time was spent out of the university, thanks to endless strikes. Every time the students staged a strike to express their grievances, the government would send the General Service Unit (GSU), a paramilitary unit of the Kenyan police force, to beat them up and spray them with teargas.

Sometimes the officers came on horses and whipped any student along their way. The students would fight back, throwing stones and burning vehicles on Thika road. The university would then be closed for an indefinite length of time, and the students had to vacate their rooms and wait for an announcement on the radio or TV, inviting them back.

One time, the university was closed for thirteen months. By the time they were called back, a lot of girls had fallen pregnant and given birth. Some simply never came back, preferring to get married, look for work, and for the richer ones, fly out of the country or join a private university to complete their studies.

During this time, Toni had been lucky to land a job at the Nairobi hospital, working as a receptionist for a renowned paediatrician, Dr Mugambi, a brilliant doctor who treated a lot of politicians' children. He was also a hot-headed, crazy lunatic of a boss, who drove his employees up the wall. Toni worked the phones, transferring calls that came in to the doctor, depending on how urgent they were. Toni had never trained as a telephone operator and the first months were very hard for her. Dr Mugambi didn't make her work easier because he was choleric, and unpredictable.

"No phone calls for me today. None, not even one, I have too much work", he instructed Toni one morning, as soon as he walked into the clinic.

She worked from a back office, which also served as the tea room, where the doctor came for his coffee break. Toni spent the morning patiently explaining to patients that the doctor was too busy to talk to them, but could they leave a message? He would call them back when he had a moment to spare, she would add.

Suddenly, the door to the back office flew open and Dr Mugambi barged in, shouting, "What the hell is wrong with you, Toni?"

Toni cringed, preparing herself for the worst. Dr Mugambi's outbursts were worse than her father's.

"Why did you tell Lucy that I'm too busy to talk to her? Do you want her to divorce me? Will you marry me when she leaves me?"

"But... you told me no phone calls at all," Toni stammered.

Dr Mugambi retorted, "Use your brain! My wife is not a

patient." Then he stormed out, back to his work.

One day, Toni decided she had had it with crazy Dr Mugambi. He had, as was the norm, given her contradictory instructions, and had proceeded to shout at her unfairly. When he was done screaming, Toni stood up, took her little handbag and announced, "I quit."

Dr Mugambi was caught by surprise because none of his other employees had ever reacted like that.

"I'm sorry Toni. Please don't leave," the doctor had apologised.

Toni stayed on, but when the announcement came, inviting the students to resume their lectures, she vowed never to go back to Dr Mugambi's.

A month after Toni had sat the French entry exam, her father called out to her as she walked into the house.

"Toni! Please come here."

Toni froze. Her father had put on the serious voice, the one he used when he had something important to say to her. She wracked her brain for a minute, wondering what she might have done wrong this time. She was too old to receive a beating, but she still feared her father's wrath. Sometimes she wished she was still the little girl whose only punishment was the strokes of a belt. Listening to her father's lectures about responsibility and maturity were harder to take.

"There was a letter for you in the mailbox," he announced, handing her a white rectangular envelope. "Bring me some tea before you open it."

After serving her father a mug of tea from the thermos flask, Toni tugged at the edge of the envelope, suddenly forgetting how to open it because of her nervousness. A small, colourful logo stood out on one of the corners. It said "Université de Toulouse, Le Mirail." Toni trembled as she struggled to open the letter as if it had been sealed off with super glue. It could go either way, she thought. It could be an acceptance letter or a letter of rejection. She had learned that both arrived in the same packaging and there was absolutely no way to determine which was which until you opened the envelope.

She pulled out the letter, her hands shaking and her heart beating fast. She then rushed to her bedroom, closed the door, and sat down on her bed with her palms together, praying silently in her heart. Less than half a minute later, she ran out of her room and nearly tripped on the carpet as she dashed to show her parents the letter.

"Mummy! Daddy! I'm going to France! I've been accepted! I'm going to France! Yippee! I'm going to France. F R A N C E!" She shouted as she enunciated the word, mostly because she couldn't believe it herself.

She was screaming and jumping up and down like a little girl, forgetting that she was already a "fully matured teenager" as she had liked to refer to herself during family gatherings. She was uncontrollable for a few minutes as she contemplated her childhood dream that was about to materialise, unsure if she should laugh or cry. It was unbelievable! She, who had always passed her French exams narrowly, the one who'd wondered if there could possibly be a way to inject herself with the French language, had aced the famous entrance exam that defied even teachers of French. Surely, Destiny must have wanted her to go to France.

Toni's father had not been too pleased about her going to France because of the high cost of living he had often heard about.

"Why don't you apply to a university in a francophone African country?" he had protested.

But Toni had been adamant. "I don't want to speak French with an African accent. I want to speak like Teacher Jacques, Dr Barasa or Miss Elizabeth. I'm going to France!"

Her father had then made it clear that she should not expect any financial help from her parents, should anything go wrong.

Nairobi, the Green City in the Sun

The newly-weds spent only one night at "L'Hôtel Splendide". Early the following morning, they checked out of the hotel. The old lady bid them "*Au revoir Siodame.*"

On their way to the Metro, Toni asked Edgar for the meaning of the word. It was simply "Monsieur et Madame" said quickly.

Laure's mother had been right on the money. The social worker Laure had directed them to had been extremely kind to them. She was a middle-aged African woman called Giselle, who told them that she was from Burundi.

After making a few phone calls, she found them a room in one of the university's hostels. It was a tiny room, designed to accommodate only one person, but for Toni and Edgar, it was more than enough. The room was so small that they almost had to come up with traffic rules to allow for smooth movement. They had to slide past each other and avoid moving around at the same time. One night, Edgar fell off the bed as he tried to roll over.

The bunker bed reminded Toni of Andy's room back at Kenyatta University, and the girl with the uncovered breast.

Edgar's fall tickled her, and she chuckled, saying "I wonder how guys in campus used to make love in such a small bed."

Edgar didn't think there was anything funny in him falling off the bed.

"How can you even think of sex? I think we should just stop this stupid dream and go back to Kenya!", He said angrily, as he climbed back onto the bed.

"And just how do you think we'd pay for the tickets? Have you forgotten that we sold all our wedding presents and that we're jobless?" Toni replied, sucking in air through clenched teeth.

Toni had been accepted to one of the three universities of Toulouse, Le Mirail, to pursue a "Licence de Sciences de l'Education", the equivalent of a bachelor's degree in Education.

Le Mirail was situated close to Bagatelle, where they had met Laure, on their first day.

Some of her lectures were very similar to the ones she had had in Kenyatta University: The psychology of education, the philosophy of education ... but she struggled to understand some of her lecturers' accents. Toni had expected everyone to speak like Teacher Jacques, but she soon discovered that, like back in Kenya, every region in France has its accent. In Paris, for example, people generally use "Metropolitan" French, while most Southerners, like in Toulouse, use "Meridional" French or what is commonly called "L'accent du Midi". The Southern accent has a sweet, musical sound, and often sounds like they want to add unwanted *g*s after nasal sounds, compared to the northern one which tends to drop off a few too many vowels and has more nasal sounds.

The Ancient French and Latin lectures turned out to be more daunting than Toni had anticipated. She couldn't borrow her classmates notes either, because she couldn't decipher their handwritings! The French system teaches children to write using the cursive method, while in Kenya it was the manuscript method.

Toni struggled to read the notes she borrowed and quickly gave up. Edgar had enrolled at the Alliance Française in the centre of Toulouse; his classes were easy-going and mostly conversational.

It seemed to Toni that he spent more time socialising with his classmates than learning French grammar rules.

As her father had warned her, everything in France was more expensive than in Kenya. Toni had never lived away from her parents' home and had never had to shop for groceries or household amenities. Two weeks after arriving in Toulouse, they had already spent almost all their money. To spend as little as they could on food, Toni came up with a plan.

"We'll keep the starter, the bread, and the dessert from dinner, and have them for breakfast and lunch, okay?"

Edgar, who had lost a lot of weight and was no longer the chubby boy Toni had first met, merely shrugged and said in a gloomy tone, "Toni, I don't think we'll last long in this country. Let's beg our parents to send us money for tickets. This was a bad mistake."

Toni glared at her husband.

"Edgar, I'm not going back to Kenya. I'm in France and I'm staying in France. If you want to go back to Kenya, that's your choice. I'm staying here."

They couldn't afford bus-fare, either, and they walked everywhere they needed to go. After that first ride in the Metro, on their first day in Toulouse, Toni and Edgar didn't take the Metro or bus for a whole month.

At the university, Toni often felt lost, like the main character in her favourite novel "Loice." Loice had grown up in the village and had left home for the first time, to join a posh girls' boarding school. Loice didn't know how a lot of things worked, and often made a fool of herself. Toni felt clumsy as she went about her day to day activities.

For example, on a very cold morning, Toni went to the vending machine at the university to fetch a cup of warm drinking chocolate.

She pressed the wrong buttons on the machine and used her last coin to buy a cup of iced tea instead. Another time she mistook the salad dressing with sauce and proceeded to pour it on her food and to warm it all up in the microwave.

Edgar made a few friends at the Alliance Française but meeting up with them became a problem because he never had money to go on any outings, which mostly involved a drink at a bar. He would always use the excuse "My wife is waiting for me at home", even when Toni had classes in the evening and wasn't at home.

The evenings were quiet and stressful. They didn't have a TV or a radio. The bed was too small to make love on, and any way, sex was the last thing on their minds. None of them brought up the topic up again after Edgar's fall. They lived as if they were brother and sister. They didn't kiss or hold hands any more. They would sit in silence, in the evening; Toni at the little desk under the window, studying, and Edgar on the bed, staring into space. Edgar would sigh and mutter under his breath, "I can't take this anymore."

When her periods came, Toni realized that she could not even afford sanitary pads. She didn't have any close friends she could ask, so she simply cut up a small towel she had, into washable pads.

But the fabric burnt her skin and left her with red, painful rashes on the insides of her thighs. She was so ashamed that she could not even undress in front of her husband. She had heard that the girls who grew up in the slums of Kibera and Mathare, back in Kenya, couldn't afford sanitary towels, but she had never thought about it. As she struggled to walk because of the pain between her thighs, she remembered her friend Nyawira and hoped that she had managed to leave the slum and have a decent life.

At the end of the first month, just as they had begun to panic and wonder where they would go, because they couldn't afford another month's rent, Lady Luck smiled at them. Toni landed a job as a baby sitter for a woman who, coincidentally, was also called Laure. The name seemed to be something of a lucky charm to them. Another Laure had almost miraculously turned up to rescue them from homelessness.

Toni had responded to an advert on one of the university's notice boards. A woman was looking for somebody to babysit her three year-old son, Maxime. Toni bought a phone card and called from the public phone booth.

"Can you come to my place on the 31st December?" Laure had asked in a sweet and professional voice on the other end of the line as soon as Toni had introduced herself and stated her reason for calling.

Toni and Edgar walked for nearly two hours to get to Laure's house, which was in Lardenne, close to the Blagnac airport. They had studied the map and followed the route the bus took from Le Mirail to Lardenne.

"I can't wait to taste one of these sandwiches," Toni remarked, as they walked past a bakery's window, laden with all kinds of delicious looking food. They had both had an apple and a cup of black tea for breakfast. They paused to take a breath before pressing on the doorbell.

Laure was a tall, beautiful woman with brown eyes, who looked as if she'd stepped out of a fashion magazine. She lived close to the airport because she was an air hostess for Air France. She welcomed the couple into her flat and introduced her cute blue-eyed son, Maxime, to them. She explained that she was divorced and lived alone with her son. She had a complicated work schedule and was looking for a live-in help for the nights she was away. The conversation was made easy by the fact that Laure spoke perfect English, so Edgar didn't have to translate every sentence, as he was used to.

"Well, Edgar and I are married, but I can come and live with you.

He will stay at the university hostel and we can see each other when I have a day off," Toni offered.

"Can you drive?" Laure asked.

"No, I'm sorry I can't. Edgar has a driving licence, but I don't," she said.

"Why don't both of you move in then?" Laure suddenly quipped, much to the surprise of the couple.

"I have an extra room. Edgar can drive my car when I'm not here. He can drop and pick Maxime to and from school. Toni, you can take care of the flat. How does that sound to you?"

"You mean, both of us, coming to stay here?" Toni blurted out.

"Yes, that is exactly what I mean. Would you like that?"

"Of course, we'd like that, wouldn't we Edgar?" Toni returned as she winked at Edgar.

The couple was so excited that they forgot to ask about the pay, happy to have a roof over their heads and to stay together. The thought of being separated had not pleased Edgar at all, as he later confessed.

The three months that Toni and Edgar spent at Laure's turned out to be quite an education. Laure was hardly ever at home and had pretty much left them to decide how to run the house. They had also become Maxime's parents spending nearly every moment of his waking life with them. When Laure wasn't working, she'd run off to spend her entire break with her boyfriend Pascal, who did not like Maxime one bit.

Maxime would sometimes go to his father's place for a weekend. But then his father, Yann, would almost always call on Toni and Edgar to babysit for him when he had the boy, and especially since Maxime would usually throw a tantrum, with loud wails, demanding to see Toni.

Laure never mentioned anything about the pay, especially since Toni and Edgar never brought it up. The couple felt so grateful to have free boarding, that they didn't dare to ask her for money.

They were scared she might throw them out and they would be immediately homeless. They however found solace in the fact that she left them in peace and bought food occasionally. Laure was anorexic; she hardly ate. It was a mystery how she managed to stay beautiful and healthy;

she sometimes forgot to buy food, even for her son. Toni wondered if she really loved her child.

Toni and Edgar started having sex again. At first it was awkward because Toni felt a bit guilty and had to remind herself that she was married to Edgar; that there was nothing wrong with what she was doing. The fact that it wasn't their house and that Laure could walk in on them at any time was also a hindrance. They probably made love three times in the three months they lived at Lardenne.

"Toni! Toni!" Maxime screamed from his bedroom one night. He was having one of his frequent nightmares.

"I'm coming sweetheart!" Toni shouted, as she got out of bed and ran towards Maxime's bedroom. She lifted the little boy and placed him on her laps, holding him tightly and rocking him gently.

"There," she cooed in a reassuring voice. "It was only a bad dream, don't be scared," Toni said, as she planted little kisses on his forehead. The boy instantly fell asleep and she lay him down gently, covered him with his Spiderman duvet, and planted a last kiss on his forehead. As she stood up to go back to her bedroom, she saw Laure standing at the doorway, looking like she was about to cry.

Toni had completely forgotten that Laure was home that night, one of the rare times she spent a full night in her house. She had probably had another fight with her boyfriend, Pascal. Laure had watched the whole scene and without saying a word, had turned, and walked back to her bedroom.

The following morning, as Toni was preparing breakfast and Edgar was playing with Maxime in the living room, Laure suddenly emerged and walked straight towards Toni, stopping three feet away from her. Toni assumed that Laure wanted to reach into the shelves in front of her.

"Why do you want to steal my child? Laure suddenly demanded in French, with a hint of threat in her voice. "Why does Maxime call out your name in the middle of the night, as if you were his mother? Are you planning to kidnap my child?" Laure asked, her voice rising a few octaves higher.

Toni was shocked at the outburst and raised voice. Laure had never raised her voice on Toni or even Edgar, even though they'd had one or two disagreements.

"Well, you're hardly ever home," Toni retorted. "Maxime used to call out your name in the beginning, but you were never there," she added.

Laure looked hurt by her statement and for a moment, was tongue tied. The bitter truth that Toni had just spat out hit her like a slap on the face. She walked out of the kitchen and banged her bedroom door, then threw herself on the bed to cry. From then on, Laure came home straight after work, fed her son, put him to bed and then left for Pascal's. She would also spend more nights at her house. But she'd completely stopped buying food for Toni and Edgar and the few times she spoke to them, she was rude and aggressive, as if they were unwanted visitors who had overstayed their welcome.

"Look Edgar," Toni jumped to her feet one day. "I'm out of here. I'm not spending another night in this house. I've had it!"

She brayed as she walked to their bedroom and dragged out her suitcase.

"But where will we go Toni? Why do you always expect me to follow you on your crazy whims? You made me resign from my job in Nairobi to come to France and starve to death. Just when things are looking brighter, you change your mind and decide to move.

I'm fed up with this!" Edgar was close to tears.

"Look, I'm not forcing you to come with me. Just as I did not force you to follow me to France. You can stay here if you want; I'm leaving!"

She began to throw clothes into her suitcase.

Earlier that day, on her way from the university, Toni had spoken to Giselle, the Social worker, who had promised to find them a room by the end of the day. When Laure walked in from work that evening, the couple had their belongings all packed up and were ready to leave.

"Hello. Where are we going?" She asked, in English, looking at each one of them in turns, trying to read their faces.

"Thank you for housing us for three months, Laure," Toni broke in. "Our time here is up. We're leaving today."

"But what will I do with my son?" Laure cried. "He adores you two. Are you just going to leave without any notice?"

"I'm sorry, but we are leaving, Laure. You'll do just fine," Toni said.

"You ungrateful bastards," Laure barked, realising that they were not going to change their minds.

"After all I've done for you?" She screamed.

But Toni and Edgar were already on their way to the door. They didn't look back as they walked away from Laure and left the residential building.

Chapter SEVEN

For the next five months, Toni and Edgar lived in a small room in the attic of a building in the city centre, on "La rue des Paradoux". Giselle had found them what the French call "une chambre de bonne" in one of the most expensive buildings in Toulouse. They would never have known this had it not been for the loud sighs and gaping mouths of nearly everyone who heard where they lived; people would marvel and wonder how they could afford to rent a flat in such a posh area of town.

A "chambre de Bonne" is a small, self-contained room in the attic of a building, which once served as a maid's room for bourgeois families. It was a tiny room which surprisingly was able to hold a bed, a kitchen, a toilet and a shower. The kitchenette was positioned between the shower and the toilet; a curious arrangement that made living there quite uncomfortable.

The amenities, including the kitchenette, were all partitioned by thick curtains alone, which of course kept everything away from each of the facilities, except the smell. Whenever she was cooking on their one-stove electric cooker and Edgar needed to use the toilet, Toni had to open the window and hold her breath until he had flashed the toilet. This prompted a rule that no one was to use the toilet when the other was preparing food in the kitchen. The shower, on the other hand, was so tiny that one could hardly afford the luxury of turning around to soap oneself. Their bed was on the other side of the room with their suitcases-cum-wardrobe under it.

During Summer, the temperatures in Toulouse can shoot up to 40°C without the hint of a breeze. Toni and Edgar's flat up in the attic was a mini-furnace, and they spent most of their evenings strolling aimlessly in the streets of the city centre, marvelling at the prices of things, and wondering if they would one day afford to buy anything.

The 1998 World cup had just kicked off and the whole of France was in a frenzy. There was a huge screen by the Garonne river, which splits Toulouse into two. Toni and Edgar spent some evenings at the Garonne, watching Zinedine Zidane and his teammates make history with their victories.

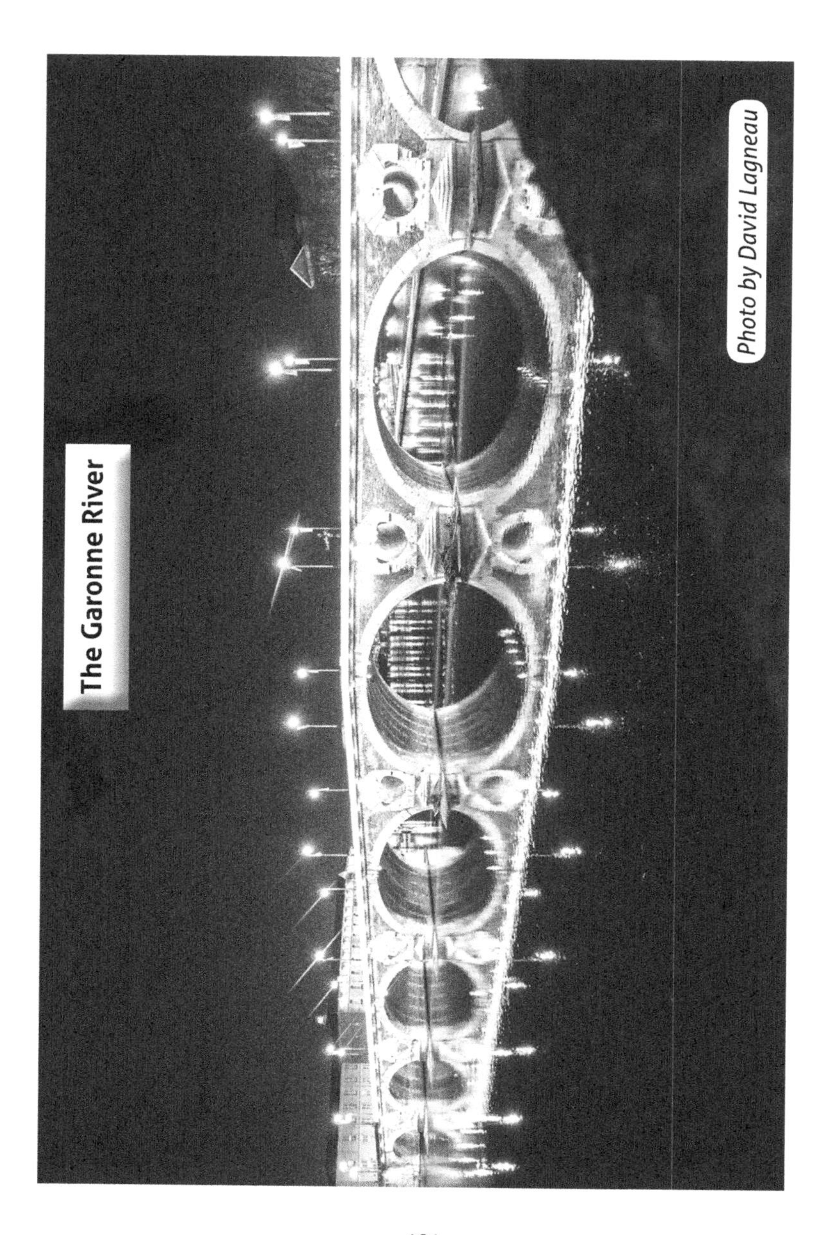
The Garonne River
Photo by David Lagneau

Giselle had been extremely generous and understanding. Was it because she came from Burundi and had probably walked in their shoes? She had paid the deposit required for the room, and one month's rent. She had also given them coupons for free food from the "Secours Populaire," which gave out relief food and clothes to immigrants and refugees in a precarious situation.

"You have to look for work because I can only pay one month's rent. After that you're on your own," she had warned them.

Every week, they went to the "Secours Populaire" to fetch free cans of food, packets of rice, flour, and a bottle of cooking oil. There was also a clothing department where they could fit some second-hand clothes and take them away, for free. For the homeless, there were free showers and even a free hairdresser. Toni made friends with a girl from Congo called Eugénie who was studying law. She told Toni that her father was a minister in their country, which baffled Toni because ministers were rich, as far as she knew.

One evening, Toni and Edgar were strolling on the "Rue de Couteliers", which was right behind "La rue des paradoux", where they lived.

"Edgar, look!" Toni pointed to the huge sign that read: LE BAGAMOYO (restaurant Africain).

The only African restaurant they had seen was the "African queen" which was on "La rue des paradoux". Hawa, the Malian woman who ran the restaurant was very kind, but she couldn't give Edgar and Toni a job because her restaurant was too small. She did everything herself: Cooking, serving, washing up and cleaning up.

They knew that Bagamoyo was a town in Tanzania, but to see the name in the heart of Toulouse was surprising. There was a big glass door with posters stuck on it. Some were adverts for African concerts and festivals around Toulouse. A roughly handwritten sign said, "Dogs are not allowed here".

Edgar pushed the door open and the couple walked in. The restaurant was empty, but there was some soft music playing in the background. There was a bar to the right, stocked with all sorts of drinks, but mostly rum. Rum from La Martinique, La Guadeloupe, La Réunion. On the wall a lot of postcards hung, yellow with age. There was a photo of a black man with a wide grin and a huge sign that said, "We only accept cheques and cash". Five small sculptures of jazz musicians, playing the trumpet, saxophone and drums stood on a shelf. A wooden staircase led to what must have been the downstairs or the basement. On one side was a brick wall, with the red Toulouse bricks showing and a huge painting of Nelson Mandela that covered half the wall. On the opposite wall, which was cemented and painted white, was a big Batik painting of a Maasai woman, carrying a baby on her hip.

Long tables ran the length of the two walls, with a long bench on either side. The lighting was soft and welcoming.

"*Bonsoir mes amis*!" A deep voice startled the couple.

An African man of medium height appeared from nowhere. He had very dark skin and a wide smile that made Toni and Edgar feel immediately at home.

"How may I help you?" He asked as he extended his right hand to Edgar. Edgar explained, in French, that they were students looking for jobs.

"Where do you come from?" George, for that was his name, asked in perfect English, which took the couple aback. How had he guessed they were anglophone?

"I can tell you're from an English-speaking country," he added with a hearty laugh.

"We come from Kenya", Toni replied, glad that she could participate in the conversation without difficulty.

"Oh! Oh! Oh!" exclaimed the man, clapping his hands and reaching forward to give Toni and Edgar a warm hug each, as they stood there, perplexed.

"Nyinyi ni ndugu zangu jamani! Walahi!" He broke out in Swahili. "You are my brother and sister! I swear!

George, the owner of Le Bagamoyo, was thrilled to meet Kenyans. He told Toni and Edgar that his parents were from Cameroon, but he was born in Tanzania and had grown up in the town of Bagamoyo, hence the name of his restaurant.

"Please give me your phone number and I'll call you as soon as I have a *kibarua* for you."

"Errrmmm..." Edgar began, in an apologetic voice. "We don't have a phone yet."

George immediately understood where they were coming from. It took him back to his first years as a student in Toulouse. "No problem. Pass by the restaurant every day at 6.00pm. We'll find something for you," he reassured the couple.

As they turned to leave, George said, "Hey, you can't leave without having something to eat! The chef will be here soon. Please, be my guests. What would you like to drink, as we wait?" He went to the bar and came back with three bottles and three glasses. A beer for himself and two coca-colas for the couple. As he poured out the drinks, he engaged in a chitchat. "My closest friend at the University of Le Mirail was a Kenyan. I really miss him. He is now a French lecturer in Nairobi. Ah.... Barasa and I had so much fun together.".

Toni almost choked on her coca-cola. "Dr Barasa? Oh my God! He was my lecturer at Kenyatta University and he's the one who recommended Toulouse to me!"

Three days later, Edgar started work in the kitchen of Le Bagamoyo. He became the official dishwasher. There was another student, Charlie, from Madagascar, who was "the chef". The menu at Le Bagamoyo was very simple: meat balls, blood sausage or chicken thighs served with rice. All cooked in the microwave. All the employees of Le Bagamoyo were students, mostly Africans.

A few weeks after Edgar began working at the restaurant, George offered Toni a job as a waitress. The beginning was tough because of her poor French, but George was a patient boss and always came to her rescue whenever she was stuck. He treated her like a daughter and never allowed any of the patrons to bully her.

George was a warm, generous host who knew all his regular customers by name. Most of the customers were students, who came for the cheap but delicious dishes, and also for the ambience. Sometimes there were so many customers that there was a long queue outside and George had to call on extra waiters and waitresses.

African music blasted from the old speakers. Musicians like Koffi Olomide, Mbilia Bel, Fela Kuti, all were played there, as was Salsa and Zouk from the West Indies. The merrier the customers became, thanks to the cheap alcohol, the more Le Bagamoyo turned into a discotheque.

When the food service was done, the waiters would push the tables against the walls and the corridor between transformed into a dance floor. George would teach Toni and the other girls how to dance Zouk. He was very protective of his girls and would quickly intervene if any of the male customers tried anything fishy. "Leave my daughters alone!" He would growl, and if the customer persisted, he would call the bouncer and instruct him to throw the customer out.

At the end of every evening, after he had made enough cash, he gave out free bottles of the cheap punch that he prepared every day.

Le Bagamoyo saved Toni and Edgar's lives; they could now afford to pay rent and buy some of the things they needed – like a phone. The restaurant only opened in the evenings, so they could comfortably attend their classes during the day.

Toni and Edgar had been living at the "Chambre de bonne" for five months when Toni suggested they move out.

"Edgar, we should apply for one of the council flats in Le Mirail. I hear they're cheap and spacious. I'm fed-up with this hole."

"They'd never accept our application," Edgar replied. "We don't even have a guarantor".

"We can ask George, I'm sure he'll agree," Toni replied.

"I doubt it. You ask him if you want, I won't bother," Edgar said.

"Do you ever do anything? I always have to ask...." Toni began. Edgar stood up and walked out of the flat. He hated confrontation and had resorted to walking out any time they had a disagreement.

"Coward," Toni muttered under her breath. She would apply for the council flat and move out alone, if she had to. She didn't care. Sometimes she wondered which devil had driven her to getting married so young.

Toni's application was accepted much to Edgar's surprise. They moved into a spacious two-bedroomed flat, with a balcony and large French windows that brought in a lot of light and a cool breeze in the summer. It was at La Reynerie, one of the estates that made up "Le Mirail" sector. The other two were Bagatelle (where they had met the first Laure), and Bellefontaine. It was rated one of the most unsafe places to live in Toulouse because of the high crime rate. Majority of the inhabitants of Le Mirail were immigrants; Arabs from North Africa and Blacks from West Africa.

Toni's first and only friend at La Reynerie, was her neighbor Sandrine, who lived with her father. The two girls had met at the university, where they were taking the same course. Sandrine wasn't an immigrant, but her parents were from a modest family.

Her mother was in a mental health facility. She suffered from schizophrenia and had tried to stab her husband on several occasions.

One summer night, when she was quietly relaxing in the house, Toni heard what sounded like a commotion outside and people shouting. She stood up and rushed towards the large French windows that led to their tiny balcony. Then she heard a loud bang and saw flames of fire rising from the parking lot downstairs.

A few Arab boys were running everywhere, throwing glowing objects at the cars parked for the night. Toni would later learn that the objects were Molotov cocktails.

"Our car!" Toni thought in horror. They had saved for months before they could acquire their very own old Ford Fiesta. Toni could only hope and wish that Edgar had taken it to work that night. He often opted to take the Metro into town for work, because it saved him the trouble of looking for parking. Toni tried to peer through the flames, desperately trying to make out if their Ford Fiesta was among the burning ones. But the smoke clouded everything, and she shut the windows in frustration and went back into the house. Fortunately, Edgar had taken the car to work that day.

Despite all the crazy happenings of Le Mirail, Toni didn't feel particularly scared living within the area. At any rate, she felt safer than when she had lived in Nairobi, where even public transport was a hellish affair. She was happy to wear her watch openly and not have it snatched by a thief at the Githurai bus-stop, as the *matatu* stopped to pick up more passengers.

She remembered being chased across town by a pickpocket. It was back when *matatu* touts used to pack human beings into the matatus like sardines in a tin. She was with her friend David in a *matatu* from Kenyatta University to town. Toni saw a pickpocket busy at work... she glared at him and turned to David.

"Angalia huyu mwizi," (look at this thief), she said, her eyes on the pickpocket. An uneasy David told her to stop staring at him, but Toni kept on looking at the thief disapprovingly.

"Umeniona ofisini yako nikikuharibia kazi?" (Have you ever seen me in your office spoiling your job?). The thief shot back at Toni.

Unfortunately for Toni, the *matatu* forced them off near Nairobi River, a place that was not only unsafe but also far from the city centre. The pickpocket chased Toni and David all the way to the city centre, shouting insults at them. *"Faga! Nisiwashike!"* (Buggers! Let me not catch you!)

The young Arab boys at Le Mirail who cat-called and whistled as girls passed by were, as far as she was concerned, harmless to her. In any case, they only bullied the French girls – not blacks like her. This was a silent code between immigrants. They referred to her as "cousin" even though she was neither Arab nor Moslem. Sandrine, on the other hand, was scared silly of them. She was often on the receiving end of insults like *"Khinzir!"* (Pig!) from the young Arabs. She however, felt safer when she was with Toni, and had taken to asking her black friend to accompany her whenever she needed to take the Metro.

After a couple of weeks at Le Bagamoyo, Toni found two cleaning jobs: one at an engineering school, early in the mornings, and another at a bank, in the evenings. So, she quit working at Le Bagamoyo, except on special occasions when George needed extra help.

"Putting all their eggs in one basket" by working at the same place with Edgar was risky. What if Le Bagamoyo closed? She had vowed never to find herself in the same precarious situation they had been in before.

The two cleaning jobs both suited Toni because they allowed her to attend her lectures during the day. She caught the first Metro out of Le Mirail, into town, at 4.30am. She put on her blue coat and cleaned toilets and classrooms before the engineering students started trickling in at 8.00am. She rushed back home, showered, and changed before going to the university for her classes. As soon as her classes were done, she jumped into a bus and went to her second job, cleaning at the bank.

When Toni met Noelle, they immediately hit it off. Noelle, who came from Togo, was a slim and beautiful girl with short natural hair, unlike many of the other West African girls who preferred weaves and applied their make-up with a shovel. She went to the American University in Toulouse. The two girls met at the engineering school, where they both cleaned before going for their classes at their respective universities.

Toni admired a lot of things about Noelle: The way she was bubbly and laughed at anything, the way she spoke both French and English fluently, but especially the fact that she drove herself around and did not have to take the Metro or the bus. Toni would watch her drive in for work, mesmerised at the sight of an African girl who seemed to have it all together. At the time, the idea of owning or driving a car was just as achievable for Toni as a swim across the Indian Ocean.

Noelle was the first African girl Toni had seen driving on the streets of Toulouse.

"Toni, why don't you learn how to drive? It would make your life so much easier," Noelle advised one day as they walked to the parking lot.

The suggestion sparked off an interest in Toni. At the end of their job, when Noelle dropped her off at the Metro stop, Toni observed keenly as Noelle switched gears and manoeuvred her way through the traffic.

A few weeks later, Toni enrolled into one of the driving schools in Le Mirail, which was run by an enthusiastic Arab man. One had to first learn "The Driving Code" then take an exam before getting anywhere near a car. As a result, one had to attend a few classes at the school, watch some DVDs then take a multiple-choice quiz. Only when you passed the code, were you allowed to take the main driving test.

The code was ideally not such a hurdle if you could read and interpret some of the signs and instructions. But Toni's French was still below average, and she flunked the code on her first two attempts. It was a 40-question quiz. One needed to get at least 35 questions right to attain the pass mark. Toni got 31 questions correctly on her first attempt. Returning with determination for the second attempt, she got 34 questions right.

Toni later discovered that some of the driving schools thrived on failed tests. They deliberately refused to prepare their students properly, by showing them only a limited number of DVDs and sample questions, so that they kept coming back to pay for more lessons.

As much as they were doing better financially, Toni and Edgar were awful in marriage. They hardly saw each other. He worked at Le Bagamoyo every day until 2.00am. By the time he came home, Toni was asleep because she had to be up at 4.00am to go to her cleaning job at the engineering school.

The rare times they tried to make love, it was a painful ordeal for Toni. Her husband never took the time to prepare her for intercourse; he would rub her clitoris roughly with one hand, before thrusting his huge penis into her. She couldn't wait for him to stop pumping her as if she were a rubber doll. It reminded her of the joke about a woman who always said to her husband "Don't forget to cover me when you're done".

Once Edgar had ejaculated, he would roll off her and immediately start snoring. Toni's vagina always stung as if somebody had poured hot chilli sauce into it. She hated having sex. She would rush to the shower and spray cold water on her aching vagina until it cooled down.

"You're frigid. You need to consult a sex therapist," Edgar had once spat at her, when she had complained that he rushed her.

Toni often wondered what it felt like to have an orgasm. She had only read about it in books but had never experienced one.

The ringing phone jolted Toni from her thoughts.

"Hey Toni, would you like to go to a rugby match this afternoon?" Sandrine asked, excitedly.

"When did you start watching rugby?" Toni shot back sarcastically.

"My uncle gave me two complimentary tickets. Let's go! It's better than staying at home bored," Sandrine insisted. "*Allez...... S'il te plait ma chérie.*" Please.

Toni had never been to a rugby match before and had in fact, never been remotely interested in the sport, but Sandrine was probably right, and the weather was good. At the Metro stop, there were three Arab boys, about ten years old.

"These kids look too young to be taking the Metro on their own," Toni remarked to Sandrine, as the Metro came to a jarring halt and the doors slid open.

The two girls chose two seats near the exit. The small Arab boys did not enter the Metro, but as soon as the automatic doors started closing, one of them put his foot between the sliding doors and they automatically opened again.

His friends giggled. He then retreated and waited for the doors to begin closing again. The second boy then stuck his foot in and the doors slid open again. The game went on for a few minutes before Toni bolted from her seat.

"Can you stop now?" She pleaded in a firm but calm tone. "We need to go. Go and play in the park; this is not a playground."

"You're not our mother! You have no right to scold us," one of the boys replied defiantly.

Toni moved menacingly towards the entrance of the Metro, glancing at the three boys with a scowl. "Try blocking this door again and you'll see fire!" she warned.

The three boys scattered, and the Metro finally left. Sandrine was amazed.

"Wow!" she said, "I'd love to have guts like you. But I'm too scared of them. I fear they might hit me." Toni chuckled and tried to explain to a clueless Sandrine how there was mutual respect between Arabs and Blacks.

The Minimes stadium wasn't as packed as Toni had expected. Most of the spectators were men and young boys; most probably fathers with their sons, out for a Saturday outing. Even though Toulouse is known the world over for its strong fifteen-aside rugby team, the seven-aside team wasn't as good. That's why complimentary tickets to this match were easily available. Toni couldn't make head or tail of rugby rules and regulations, so she contented herself with admiring the muscular boys who were running across the field, tossing an oval-shaped ball to each other.

Their thick thighs trembled as they ran, and Toni loved the messy, boyish looks, as well as the power, speed, and agility they portrayed.

Toulouse was hosting Aix en Provence, one of the best teams in the national tournament. The result was, unsurprisingly, a staggering defeat. After the match, Toni and Sandrine followed the other spectators to the "bar," which was a make-shift building at the end of the field.

Two or three volunteers were selling lager in huge plastic tumblers. Half a pint went for three euros. They ordered a pint each. Toni nearly spat out violently when she took the first sip of the golden liquid. Her face crumbled as she tried to make out the taste of the beer, which was somewhere between that horrible bone soup she used to have back in Kiambu, and a crushed aspirin. The skin on her throat tightened as she forced down the first few sips and she remembered Francis, Edgar's good friend that she'd known back in Kenya. Francis claimed to love beer, but he always looked like he'd taken a gulp of quinine whenever he had one. His face would contort into an ugly mask, and his eyelids slam down completely as the bitter liquid went down his throat.

Sandrine and Toni stood at the end of counter, taking occasional deep draughts of the frothy fluid, glancing around furtively as if they were in a foreign country. They had placed their handbags on the counter, next to the wall. There weren't many women there and Toni felt a bit out of place, being the only black. A huge man stood next to her and she could feel his eyes poring onto her. She wished they could move away to another spot, but that was the only free space and she didn't want to balance her beer and her handbag as the pub was filling up quite fast.

The huge man standing next to Toni had black curly hair and wore a cream trench coat. When he sipped his beer, some of the foam stayed on his moustache. He would then gently lick it off and take another sip. This made Toni's stomach turn. She found him very ugly. Looking at him didn't make her beer taste any better.

"Hi, you're very cute. Where do you come from?" He suddenly piped up, jolting her so that she nearly spilled her beer.

She glanced at him and with her faulty French mumbled, "Thank you. I come from Kenya."

Toni's hopes that he would end it there were quashed. He looked too old to be chatting up a young girl like her. She turned her back to him and rolled her eyes at Sandrine, who got the message she was trying to relay without words.

"Let's go," Sandrine said, picking up her handbag from the counter.

"Yes, let's go," Toni agreed.

She took one last sip of the bitter liquid, cringed as it slid down her throat, and grabbed her handbag from the edge of the counter.

"Hey! *Mesdemoiselles*, wait. Don't leave just yet," one of the bartenders called out.

He placed two fresh tumblers full of beer in front of them just as they turned around to leave.

"Excuse-me, there's been a mistake," Sandrine said in a regretful tone to the bartender, who had already turned to serve another patron.

"Oui Mademoiselle?" he said as he raised his eyebrows with a slight nod. "Yes, young lady?"

"But we have not ordered these beers," Sandrine explained to the bartender, who was now smiling and glancing at the huge guy standing next to Toni.

"This gentleman ordered the beers for you girls," he said with a nod towards the huge guy.

They didn't feel like taking another half-pint of bitter beer, but it would be rude to turn him down.

Toni grabbed her tumbler, raised it to him and said, *"Merci Monsieur."*

"Please, call me Jean-Pierre," he said.

A strange thought whizzed by Toni's mind that she almost giggled. His voice reminded her of Don Williams, the country singer.

"Toni," Sandrine blurted out, "Please watch my beer and my bag, I need to use the bathroom," she said as she walked off. Toni was left with no choice but to chat with Jean-Pierre for whatever amount of time Sandrine would be gone. Jean-Pierre then launched into an endless line of inquiry, assailing her with questions about herself, why she had come to Toulouse, and what she studied. Toni answered him politely but side-stepped the little piece of information that she was married. He told her he was a commander in the police, but Toni didn't believe him at first.

"You're lying; show me your ID," she said, then wished she could take back her words.

The last time she had questioned the identity of a police officer in casual wear, she had spent a whole day in a cell at the Korogocho Police station in Nairobi. But Jean-Pierre was already reaching into his wallet. Toni was surprised when she saw a photo of him as a young man. There was an almost night and day difference between the man in front of her and the man on the picture. The young Jean-Pierre was handsome, with eager, keen blue eyes. Jean-Pierre also pulled out a business card from his front pocket and handed it to her.

"Please give me a call," Jean-Pierre said. "I will try get you a better job than the cleaning one."

Toni's eyes brightened. She was tired of her cleaning jobs, even though the only jobs easily accessible to students at the time were cleaning or babysitting jobs. She had tried babysitting, but her lectures at the university usually ran past 4.30pm, the time a babysitter is required to pick up children from school.

Chapter EIGHT

Toni was alone at home. Edgar had gone out to the shops, but he had said he wasn't going to be long. That's when her parents called: Her brother Ken was missing, and they were worried. Hours earlier, a bomb had gone off in Nairobi. It was August 7th, 1998. Around 4.00pm.

Toni went into panic. They didn't have a TV, so she had no means of keeping abreast with the news, and she couldn't afford to spend any more time on the phone. When Edgar walked in, about an hour later, he found a hysteric Toni waiting for him.

"Where have you been? People are dying in Kenya and you don't even care!" Toni screamed.

"How did you expect me to know?" Edgar asked nonchalantly.

"You're a selfish bastard who only thinks about himself!" Toni spat out.

Edgar didn't walk out this time. He moved towards Toni, drew back his right hand, and slapped her hard on her left cheek, sending her reeling to the floor.

"You'll pay for this, I promise you! I'm leaving you! You're a monster!" Toni screamed.

Edgar went into the kitchen and came back with the jug of cold water they always left on the kitchen table. He emptied its contents on Toni's head, without a word, and walked out of the flat.

Toni decided to skip class that day, but of course didn't tell Edgar where she would be going. The marriage was clearly on life support, since the day he'd slapped her and poured water on her. She had sworn never to have sex with him again. She regretted marrying him and wished she had come to France alone.

She wore her orange and grey Scottish skirt which she had bought with her first pay at the Bagatelle flea market. It had been very cheap, but she loved the way it hugged her narrow hips and made her look and feel feminine. On top, she put on a grey sweater with a polo neck. They looked very fine together, she thought. Her hair was in braids, thanks to Eugénie, her Congolese friend. She held them back with a rubber band and applied a little make-up.

Jean-Pierre had asked her to take the Metro up to Jolimont, he would be waiting at the parking lot downstairs. There was a staircase that led to the outside parking lot. Jean-Pierre was waiting in his long, silver Renault. He flashed the lights as soon as she appeared. Toni could hear his heavy breathing as he turned to peck her on the cheek.

"I've booked a table at a friend's restaurant," he announced, as he clipped his safety belt on. "I hope you'll like it".

A French restaurant? Toni thought. She had never been to a French restaurant in the one-and-a-half years she'd spent in Toulouse. The only restaurant she knew was Le Bagamoyo.

The restaurant was about ten minutes away from Jolimont. Jean-Pierre found a slot in the parking just in front of the restaurant. Toni was glad they didn't have to walk far. She wasn't very comfortable being seen with this huge, old man. Jean-Pierre was only forty eight, but at her young age of twenty-five, Toni found him ancient.

Aldo, the restaurant owner, was Italian, and about Jean-Pierre's age. He was a lanky figure with a loud raucous voice that stunned Toni when he spoke. He shook Jean-Pierre's hand warmly and merely nodded at Toni. With a sweep of his hand, he showed them to their table and beckoned one of the waiters to take their order.

Toni couldn't tell what all the dishes on the menu were. She was relieved when Jean-Pierre suggested the day's specialty, which was "Boeuf Bourguignon", a traditional French dish made of beef cooked in red wine. Jean-Pierre chose an "Entrecôte" steak for himself.

"My friend, might you have a small job for this young lady?" Jean-Pierre asked Aldo, who had come to join them at their table. All the other patrons had left, and the restaurant was calm.

"Sure," Aldo remarked, scanning Toni as if he was seeing her for the first time. "When can you come for a trial session? Have you ever worked in a restaurant?"

"I have only worked in an African restaurant, but I am willing to try," Toni replied in her bad French.

"Fine," he said. "You can start next week. Be here at eleven o'clock on Monday," he ordered.

"Merci monsieur," Toni returned.

A few days later, Jean-Pierre picked Toni from Jolimont as planned. As soon as he arrived, Toni walked towards the car, cast furtive glances around before quickly slipping into the car as if it was a getaway car. She was nervous about being spotted by anyone who knew Edgar.

Jean-Pierre leaned over and covered her mouth with saliva, before driving off excitedly. He lived in a village called Lespinasse, situated in the outskirts of Toulouse and about twenty minutes by car. They listened to the News on the Radio, and then switched to "Nostalgie", the station that played strictly oldies. Jean-Pierre hummed along to Claude François, JacquesBrel, Joe Dassin and other musicians from his youth. The only song she recognised was "Alexandrie, Alexandra" of Claude François, because one of her lecturers at Kenyatta University had made them learn it.

Toni knew they had reached Lespinasse from the sign at the entrance of the village. After crossing a small green bridge with flower pots hanging by the side, she stretched out to look out the window and saw a river gushing by. Jean-Pierre explained that it was called "The Save" and that it was a part of "The Garonne", which ran from Toulouse to Bordeaux. Toni nodded in acknowledgment and mock interest although she wasn't very interested in Geography.

The Renault swerved as Jean-Pierre made a sudden left turn after the sign as if it was a last-minute decision, then a right at the next roundabout. Nearly all the houses in the area had been built on expansive land. He pressed on a remote and the brown gate opened automatically. They drove in and stopped in front of a garage which was shut.

"Welcome home," Jean-Pierre said and turned off the ignition, before struggling to heave his mass out of the car. The door cracked opened and two huge, black Rottweilers emerged. They bolted towards their master, wagging their tails, with their big pink tongues hanging out and licking him everywhere. Toni clutched onto Jean-Pierre's arm in fear and almost let out a scream when one of the monsters made a lunge at her to sniff her.

"Don't be scared," he said reassuringly as he stroked each of them. "They're very kind. Hugo! Olympe! Back in the house. Now!" He ordered. The dogs obeyed and led them into the house. Toni trudged slowly behind Jean-Pierre, still holding his hand tightly. She felt relieved when they finally went into the house and the two monsters, who seemed to follow each other all the time, disappeared.

A young beautiful woman sat on a chair at the dining room table as Toni walked in. She was feeding a baby from a bottle and looked up as they came in, sneered, and continued feeding her baby.

"Toni, meet Isabelle, my daughter," Jean-Pierre volunteered. Toni didn't know what to do; stretch out her arm or just say hello. She immediately felt intimidated by this girl who had a freezing cold stare.

"You didn't say you were bringing anybody home for lunch," she hissed. Jean-Pierre removed his jacket and threw it on one of the sofas, which was already laden with clothes.

"This is my house, I bring whoever I want, whenever I want," he said.

Isabelle stood up and carried the baby out of the room, with a click of her tongue. She disappeared into a corridor that Toni assumed led to the bedrooms, before slamming a door so hard, that one of the dogs barked loudly. Toni was shocked by the hostility that transpired between Isabelle and her father. It was as if the air had suddenly become heavy and wet with vendetta.

She would later learn that Jean-Pierre was still angry that Isabelle had become pregnant so young, and that she was going out with a Gypsy who lived in a caravan. According to Jean-Pierre, the Gypsy was just another hoodlum out to ruin his daughter's life. Isabelle, on the other hand, was a sworn rebel, and couldn't give two hoots in hell what her father thought.

Isabelle, aged eighteen, had one brother, Léo, aged twelve. He looked a lot like his sister but was friendlier towards Toni. Their mother, estranged from their father, had passed away from cancer when Léo was only eight.

From the photos she saw later, Toni could tell that they had taken their good looks from their deceased mother. She had been a beautiful, tall, black woman from the French West Indies, La Martinique.

"Léo, this is my friend Toni", said Jean-Pierre, to a young man who had entered the room.

"Nice to meet you Toni", Léo said as he planted a kiss on each of her cheeks, a normal gesture in France but one which made Toni relax, after the cold treatment from Isabelle.

She immediately liked Léo. He had a warm smile and sparkling eyes. Isabelle and her father could have easily featured in a box office family drama movie.

Toni learnt from Jean-Pierre that after the death of her mother, Isabelle, who had only been a teenager, had started keeping very bad company; hanging out with, as Jean-Pierre described them, delinquents, losers, and weed smokers from the ghettos in Paris, where they lived at the time.

Isabelle had got pregnant and had had to drop out of school before obtaining her Baccalauréat, the high school certificate. She had messed up her entire life, as far as Jean-Pierre was concerned, and he took every opportunity to remind her, with insults and criticism. Isabelle didn't take it all lying down, she hit back hard, and way below the belt.

"Isabelle, you're worse than a prostitute. You spread your legs for poor gypsies who can't even buy you a coffee," Jean-Pierre would curse vehemently.

"I'd rather spread my legs for a poor gypsy than for an old filthy sod like you," she would snarl back.

Most evenings, Isabelle would head out after dinner. She would feed her baby, put him to bed and then leave to spend the evening with her boyfriend. She would ask Léo to watch over her baby while she was away. Jean-Pierre hated it. He wanted her to stay home with her child, not spend evenings smoking marijuana with her friends. But Isabelle had threatened to move out to the caravan with her boyfriend, if he as much as attempted to stop her.

One evening, as Isabelle was about to walk out, Jean-Pierre shouted after her.

"I hope you didn't wear any knickers, you whore. That way it will go in faster."

Isabelle did not answer this time, which baffled Toni. She simply turned and walked back to her bedroom, as if she had forgotten something important and was going back for it. Less than a minute later, she charged out of her bedroom, nostrils flaring, and teeth bared. She was pointing a gun at her father.

"Look what I stole from you, you old sod. Leave me alone or I will shoot you and your stupid girlfriend or report to the authorities that you, a commander of the police," she said as if he was no such thing, "has lost a gun."

Toni held her breath and shut her eyes and waited for a loud bang. She wished they'd just go back to their crazy arguments and insults. This was becoming too much. But Jean-Pierre didn't seem to panic.

"Put that gun back where you found it, you idiot," he barked.

"It's not loaded so you can't shoot me with it. If you report me, I'll arrest you for theft and you can rot in jail, as your bastard of a son is brought up by the social workers."

The scuffle was over before Toni could even make out what was really happening. Did a young girl just pull a gun on her father and threaten to kill him? She couldn't believe that even though a gun was not exactly pointed at her, she had been on the brink of witnessing a shooting incident. The thought sent a chill through her, but little did she know that it was not the last time.

Every time Toni came around, the air in the room would become taut with tension and Isabelle and Jean-Pierre would soon be hurling insults at each other.

Jean-Pierre was a wonderful cook, Toni quickly found out. The first time he had invited her over for lunch, they had eaten prawns for starters and a "Coq au vin" for the main dish. Jean-Pierre excitedly explained how he had prepared it the previous night, because it tasted better when kept overnight.

Léo demonstrated how one scooped a bit of butter with a prawn, dipped it into raspberry-flavoured vinegar, and then dropped it whole, into the mouth in a neat, swift gesture. Isabelle hadn't bothered to join them for lunch.

After the lunch, Jean-Pierre suggested, "Chérie, let's go and take a short siesta, to help us digest the food."

Léo had already disappeared into his bedroom. Toni didn't like the way Jean-Pierre called her "Chérie," as if she was his girlfriend. She wished he'd drop it but didn't know how to tell him. She timidly followed him to his bedroom, which was at the end of the corridor. On the right was Isabelle's bedroom while Léo's bedroom was on the opposite side. The corridor was dark, and the smell of dogs rent the air. Olympe and Hugo lived in the house with Jean-Pierre and his children. Hugo, the male, weighed a whole ninety kilos and had a huge head that seemed heavier than it could carry. Olympe, who Toni learnt was Hugo's mother, was smaller and had a gentler look. Toni had heard that Rottweilers were very dangerous dogs and that it was obligatory to use a muzzle on them in public places.

Jean-Pierre pushed the bedroom door open and fumbled for the light switch. The blinds were drawn so the room was in total darkness. Toni scanned the room which was about ten metres squared. It was in a mess. Clothes were strewn on a chair by the window and there was a raft of papers and boxes on the floor. Adjacent to the bedroom was a small bathroom with a shower and a sink, but no toilet.

"Get out of here, you idiot!" Jean-Pierre screamed at Olympe, who had followed them into the bedroom.

He kicked the door shut and took off his t-shirt, panting at the slight effort. He sat on the edge of the bed and bent down to undo his laces. His breathing was loud and heavy; like those old lorries that struggled to climb Thika Road, back in Kenya. When the laces came undone, he straightened his back and kicked off his shoes.

Standing up, he reached for his belt and loosened it. He fumbled for a minute with the buttons of his jeans before finally peeling it off, revealing a pair of snow-white boxers.

Toni gaped at the spectacle, her lips slightly parting. Save for his underwear, he was completely undressed. She had never seen a naked white man before. His skin looked so.... strange. She didn't know what to make of it. He then plonked himself onto the bed, which responded with a sad creak, as if it was complaining.

Toni was nervous, not knowing what to do next or what was expected of her.

"Come and lie down beside me, Chérie," Jean-Pierre offered, patting the empty side of the bed.

Toni slowly removed her shoes and lay stiffly next to him, fully clothed, and with every muscle tightened.

"Come on sweetie, you can't take a nap with your clothes on," he brayed. "Take them off, you'll be more comfortable." Toni obeyed, and with much reluctance, slowly peeled off her skirt and top as if they had been glued to her skin earlier that morning. Oh shit! She was wearing her old, brown grandma knickers. Had she known that she was going to get undressed, she would have worn one of her prettier lace panties. But it was too late now, she was already undressed.

She slipped under the duvet, hoping he would fall asleep fast and not notice her embarrassment. As she lay down with her back to him, she noticed that he was lying on his back, with his huge belly spread out like an inflated balloon at the beach. One pop using a sharp pin and the huge belly would deflate like a basketball, she thought.

She closed her eyes and pretended to sleep, but Jean-Pierre was already breathing heavily, his eyes were closed. He must be asleep, she thought. She quietly turned to face the ceiling and opened her eyes to steal a side glance. He was quite fat, and he must have weighed over a hundred kilos, she thought. Toni liked tall men, not as short as her husband, but even though he was tall, Jean-Pierre was overweight, surely. She turned to face the other side of the bed and wondered for a moment how she'd ended up in his bed, now almost naked.

She stirred when Jean-Pierre suddenly rolled over to his left side, so that he was now facing her. He placed a hand on her waist and pulled her closer to him, her back now touching his belly. She could feel his breath on her neck and began to feel his fingers slithering up and down her right thigh. She wanted him to stop, but she felt powerless, so she let him go on. After all, she hadn't felt the strong hold of a man in many months and soon began to realize how much she'd missed it.

Two fingers slowly slipped under the hem of her ugly knickers and run up and down her clitoris. Her head wanted him to stop but her body wanted other things. She didn't resist when he suddenly and urgently pulled her knickers down without saying a word. His breathing had gone up a couple of knots and Toni could now feel the warmth of his breath on her back as he continued to caress her ever so gently. She started feeling warm all over and her pussy was soon soggy and dripping wet, her clitoris throbbing like a heart inside a chest. He shoved the duvet to the side and rolled her over to her back.

"Let me lick your pretty pussy sweetheart," he mumbled, almost inaudibly, as he knelt in front of her.

"Yes, kind sir, please do," she thought but did not say a word.

Her husband had licked her once or twice, hurriedly. She had loved the sensations it had given her, but she had been too shy to ask him to continue.

Jean-Pierre parted her legs wide and dove in, lapping at her clitoris as if it was an ice-cream. Toni let out a loud gasp before quickly covering her mouth with her hand, ashamed that she was enjoying this so much. She was now reduced to faint and stifled moans, whimpering as he licked her up gently. He then stuck two fingers into her pussy and began an up and down rhythm that was in tandem with his tongue on her clit. Toni felt like she was going to explode in his face. Then he stopped suddenly and went back to lying on his back.

"Come and ride me," he whispered into her ear, nibbling it softly with his teeth.

He lifted her almost effortlessly with both hands and gently eased his stiff penis into her, planting little kisses on her neck as he rocked her up and down in irregular motions. It felt like being on top of a huge, cuddly, teddy bear. His skin was as soft as his penis was hard, probing her, as if it was on a treasure hunt.

"Take your time. Savour him, he's all yours, Ma chérie," Jean- Pierre whispered.

Toni had never felt anything like that before. It was as if she was a virgin all over again as Jean-Pierre's penis rubbed her in all the right places, setting off all sorts of wonderful sensations inside her whole body. She closed her eyes and let herself go with a man whom, only a few moments ago, she was quite certain she didn't like.

Something strange was happening, something new even, she thought. Whatever it was, it was heightening with every thrust he gave, and she couldn't hold it any longer. She erupted into a series of short convulsions before a scream let itself out of her mouth.

She couldn't control herself. Her body went into convulsions. Jean-Pierre continued rocking her, up and down, as she continued screaming and repeating "Oh my god! Oh my god! Oh my god!

At twenty-five, and after two years of marriage, Toni had just had her first ever orgasm. Her life would never be the same again.

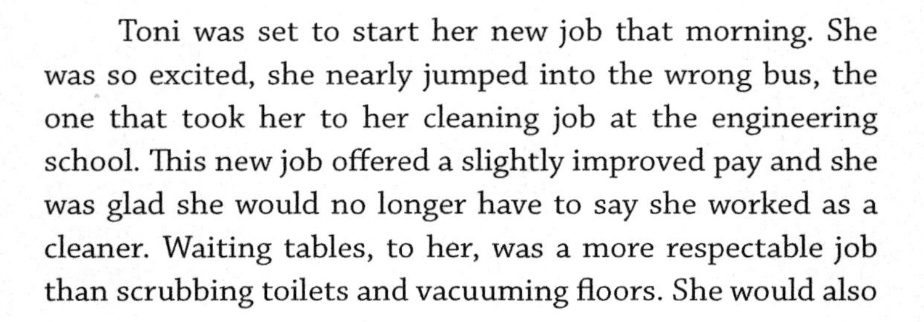

Toni was set to start her new job that morning. She was so excited, she nearly jumped into the wrong bus, the one that took her to her cleaning job at the engineering school. This new job offered a slightly improved pay and she was glad she would no longer have to say she worked as a cleaner. Waiting tables, to her, was a more respectable job than scrubbing toilets and vacuuming floors. She would also get to wear her pretty dresses and not have to cover them with that ugly, blue coat she loathed.

Toni arrived at the restaurant at exactly 11am, as instructed by Aldo, the day he had agreed to hire her. She was received by Aldo's partner, Cécile, who told her more about the job.

"This is how you set the forks and the knives, the salt and the pepper, and the table cloth," she instructed.

She taught Toni how to cut the Baguette, the long French bread: two and a half slices for each customer so that there wouldn't be any wastage at the end of the day. The first lessons were quickly over, and she sent Toni to the back room near the kitchen so that she could have lunch and prepare herself before the patrons started coming in.

Despite the small size of the restaurant, Cécile warned her that there would be a lot of work. Alessandro, the chef, came into the backroom with two plates and handed Toni one of them. Fifteen minutes into the meal, Aldo walked in, shouting.

"You!" Aldo said, looking in the direction of Toni. "If you want to have lunch then you have to come in a little earlier."

He had obviously forgotten that he'd asked her to come in at 11am. Toni would later learn from Alessandro that Aldo was always in a bad mood and it was best to stay out of his way. Toni would feel the poke of Aldo's eyes as she went about her daily tasks, making her so nervous during those first few days, that she was lucky she did not drop a plate or glass on the floor.

Every day, Toni had to cram the day's specialty, all

the fancy ingredients used, and be able to explain it to the customers. Her scrappy French did not make it any easier and she dreaded the request: *"Pourriez-vous me décrire le plat s'ilvous-plaît?"* (Can you tell me more about this dish?)

When all the customers had left, Toni and her colleagues would clear the tables, load the dishwashers, hoover, and mop the floors.

Aldo would put together all the tips collected during the day, count them, and then slot them into his own pocket, instead of giving them to the waiters, as other restaurants did.

"Your work is so shoddy, you don't deserve any tips," he would say to them in a dismissive tone.

Aldo was also never satisfied with Toni's reporting time and made her come in earlier each day. By her second week at Aldo's, Toni had begun regretting the decision to quit her cleaning job.

All she had had to do there was be at work on time, carry out her chores, then leave. She didn't have a crazy boss shouting at her for hours and calling her "lazy and slow." Heck – she didn't even need to speak good French to scrub the toilets!

One morning, close to tears after Aldo had yet again screamed at her, Toni stepped out of the back door for some fresh air. Alessandro was leaning against the wall, puffing on a Marlboro. He offered her a cigarette and without thinking, she grabbed it and the lighter, and lit it up. She took a long drag and what followed was the unmistakable sign of a first-time smoker; a hacking cough as smoke came out through all her cavities. Alessandro merely smiled not wanting to embarrass her with the obvious question.

A few days later, on a busy afternoon, when all the tables were occupied, and Aldo was yelling instructions and corrections at all the staff members, Toni decided she had had enough. The next morning, she didn't go to work and didn't bother calling to say why.

She ignored all of Aldo's calls, until he called Jean-Pierre.

"Tell him to go to hell," Toni cut off Jean-Pierre as soon as he'd launched the topic. "I am never going back to that restaurant."

Chapter NINE

The day after she quit her job at Aldo's, Toni headed to the Alliance Française in the centre of Toulouse. She had accompanied Edgar to the place several times and knew of the noticeboard which often had job offers for English speakers: Babysitting, giving English lessons to students, taking care of elderly people at night, cleaning, even walking dogs! One job caught Toni's attention:

"Hello! We're between two and four years old, we go to a little school called 'Ma Première Page,' and we're looking for a kind person to teach us English songs and counting. Thank you!"

There were colourful little drawings all over the page, obviously done by the little children. Toni took her new cellphone that she had bought with the money from her cleaning jobs, and dialed the number attached to the advert.

"Ma Première Page. Bonjour!" A pleasant voice answered the phone.

"*Bonjour,* I'm calling about your advert," Toni announced. "Can you come for an interview tomorrow?" The woman on the other line asked.

"Yes, I can," Toni replied.

"Great. My name is Nathalie. I can see you at 2pm when the kids are napping. Please don't forget your CV."

The following day, Toni took the Metro up to La Roseraie, home to "Ma Première Page." When she got there, she was surprised to find out that the school was in a quaint Toulousain house. The walls were made of red bricks, as well as the window frames. The shutters and door were painted blue, like many Toulouse houses. A low brick wall ran around a small garden in front of the house, with an arch in the middle, above a passage without a gate. The arch was painted with the same drawings Toni had seen on the advert, and a sign that announced, "Ma Première Page."

Toni walked the little distance from the arch to the blue door. Before she could knock or find a bell to ring, the door opened. A dark-haired woman, in her thirties, appeared at the doorway. She had long, untamed, curly black hair and kind, deep eyes. "Come in! I'm Nathalie. You must be Toni," she said, taking Toni's hand in a firm handshake.

"We'll do the interview in the kitchen because the children are taking their afternoon nap and we wouldn't want to wake them up."

They were standing in a big room with tiny benches, tables, and chairs all over. It reminded Toni of the giant stories she used to read as a child – she was the giant and she had entered the tiny elves' home. There were tiny clothes hanging on each chair and tiny pairs of shoes at the feet of the chairs.

There was also a huge green board, shaped like an apple.

"This is the 'Apple Room'. We undress the children for their afternoon nap," Nathalie explained.

The kitchen was to the left of the apple room and the décor was similar – tiny tables and chairs. There was a sink, a fridge, a dishwasher, and a laundry machine. Nathalie then led Toni out of the kitchen, past the apple room.

"Shhhhh!" she whispered, placing her pointing finger on her lips. She opened a door to the left and beckoned Toni with her hand. The room was dark, save for a nightlight on a shelf, but Toni made out many tiny mattresses on the floor. There was a little child on each mattress, covered with a tiny duvet. A woman sat in the corner, watching over the children. She waved and smiled. The other room had a low square table and the same tiny chairs. On the wall hung children's drawings. There were shelves all round, containing boxes of paint, paint brushes, felt pens, tiny pairs of scissors and rolls of paper.

The bathroom was straight out of a doll house: tiny toilets, tiny sinks, and a tiny bathtub. On a shelf was a huge pile of diapers and packets of wet wipes. Toni could smell the dirty diapers in the bin, but it wasn't as repulsive as Dr Aggrey's, she thought.

Nathalie led Toni back to the kitchen to begin the interview. She sat at one of the tables and pulled out a small chair for Toni. The interview was pleasant. Nathalie explained that she had started the little school after graduating from the university as a child psychologist. The kindergarten took in children from ages two to four. Four other girls made up the educational team and they worked in shifts, three at a time. She explained that they were looking for an English speaker to give "notions" of English to the children. Basically, teach them nursery rhymes and a few words in English. Since some of the children were young and not yet potty-trained, the job also involved changing diapers for the younger ones and helping the older ones wipe themselves clean after using the toilet. There were also the snack times (at 10.00am and 4.00pm) and the lunch meal to serve and feed the slower children. The only condition was that Toni had to speak to the children strictly in English.

After asking Toni a few questions about herself and looking through her CV, Nathalie promised to call her within a week. "I'll get back to you. I have two other candidates to interview."

A week later, Toni's phone rang.

"Happy Birthday Toni! I have good news for you – you got the job!"

For a second Toni wondered how Nathalie had known it was her birthday. Then she remembered that she had taken a copy of her CV.

Toni began her teaching job at the little school a week later. Nathalie organised a little "welcome party" for her, where she met her other colleagues, Béatrice, Colette and Martine, all in their thirties. She also met the thirty children, some of whom had never seen a black person before.

"Why do you have brown skin?" One little girl called Louise asked.

"Does everybody in your family look like you?" A little boy added.

Every morning, the teachers would gather the children

in the Apple Room and teach them songs. The teachers took turns. Toni taught the children songs like "The wheels on the bus go round and round" and "Head, shoulders, knees and toes." Each child would then pick out a card with his or her name and stick it on the magnetic green apple board. Toni taught them how to say, "My name is...."

Nathalie was a kind boss who made Toni feel at home right from the start. Béatrice was less friendly and seemed to think she spoke English better than Toni.

"The girl who worked here before you said 'Hallo' not 'Hello,'" she would say to Toni, who would patiently explain that both were correct.

Béatrice always wore her hair in a tight bun and hardly ever smiled or found anything funny. Toni wondered why she worked with children if she didn't have a sense of humour. Nathalie, on the other hand, was always making the children squeal with laughter as she told them funny stories about giants and rabbits.

Colette, who was slightly older than the other girls, was the artist of the school. She had studied fine art in college and always had creative ideas for the children to work on. For Toni's birthday, she had the children paint on wine glasses with leaves and twigs, using special paint for glass. Toni was touched that these people, who hardly knew her, could go out of their way to celebrate her birthday belatedly. Martine, her other colleague, was smack in the middle of a bitter divorce and was always complaining about her ex-husband.

Within a few weeks, the little children had come to love Toni and were excited to repeat the words and songs she taught them in English. Toni finally understood why Teacher

Jacques had been so passionate about teaching French to the children at City Primary. Thinking that some of those children would fall in love with English the way she had fallen in love with French at a tender age, and that their lives would be changed forever filled Toni's heart with much joy for the five years she worked at Ma Première Page.

Clément was a sweet, blue-eyed, three- year old boy who adored Toni and followed her everywhere. Sometimes Toni had to gently nudge him off her lap when he insisted he wanted to sit on it. His mother was expecting a second child. Nathalie had advised all the teachers to be extra gentle with him.

"Clément, what would you like to name your little brother or sister when he's born?" Nathalie asked Clément one day.

"If it's a boy, I'd like to call him 'Tom'. If it's a girl, I'd like to call her 'Claire'. If the baby is black, I'd like to call him James, because he'll speak English like Toni," Clément explained excitedly, which sent all the teachers reeling with laughter. Even Béatrice managed a smile that day.

After the morning singing session, the three teachers on shift would each take a group of ten children and have an activity with them for an hour. The activities varied from painting, colouring, cutting, and pasting. One teacher would be in the apple room, another in the painting room and yet another in the square room.

When the hour was up, and before the children had lunch, they would all gather in the napping room to listen to a story; with one of the teachers. The other two teachers would go to the bathroom and call out the children, one by one, to change their diapers or to pee, if the child was potty-trained. The children would then wash their hands and go to the kitchen for lunch.

Lunch-time was always an animated period because some of the children refused to eat some kinds of food, especially green vegetables. There was one rule: "You have to taste."

The children undressed down to their undies before going for their afternoon nap. The teachers took turns sitting in the napping room during the nap time, to ensure that no child woke the others up. During this break, the other teachers would take a coffee, have a cigarette outside, or read a book, after cleaning up the kitchen and loading the dish-washer.

Toni enjoyed the shifts she worked with Nathalie and Colette best, because they were lively and always had something to laugh about. The shifts with Béatrice and Martine were less fun, so she avoided hanging around them during the lunch break. She would always volunteer to sit in with the children. It was more fun than listening to Béatrice's endless "The girl who worked before you said... sang... pronounced...." Or to hear Martine's lamentations about her ex who had run off with another woman. Toni had her own personal problems that she only shared with Nathalie, because she felt closer to her than to the others.

It quickly dawned on Toni that studying and working in France was almost impossible. Legally, a student could only work up to twenty hours a week. For students like Toni, who had no financial help from their parents, and who had no scholarships, the money made from working twenty hours a week was not enough for rent, school fees and the other bills. A lot of foreign students, especially Africans, worked illegally for many more hours. Some had to support their families back home with the meagre salaries they earned cleaning or washing dishes in restaurants.

When Toni applied for university in France, she had a lot of ambition; she wanted to do her Masters, and even go further in her studies. But she quickly abandoned those dreams and instead concentrated on trying to get her student visa renewed each year – a difficult thing if ever there was one. To have their student visa renewed each year, students had to present proof of examination results. Luckily, the authorities did not insist on proof of attendance, so all Toni did was find out the dates of the examinations and present herself. She failed most of them because she never attended lectures. Every year she would cross her fingers and hope that the government employee would be lenient and renew her papers.

As the years passed, Toni's deportation became increasingly imminent. She had to find a way to change her status from student to worker, which would allow her a long-term visa. Nathalie, her boss, had offered to help her. If she put together a dossier, and promised to give Toni a full-time job, she was sure her status would be changed. But the authorities rejected her application, claiming that the job Toni did at Ma Première Page could be performed by a French citizen. Luckily for Toni, Jean-Pierre knew a woman who worked for the government, and through connections, he managed to have her visa renewed.

Toni was fed up with her marriage. She felt like a stranger in her own home. She had moved to the spare room, to sleep on a mattress on the floor and could hardly stand the sight of her husband, leave alone the feel of his hand on her. She had never forgiven him for the slap. He had also found out about her affair with Jean-Pierre; thanks to Sandrine, who hadn't managed to keep her mouth shut. Edgar had written to Toni's father and informed him that his daughter was having an affair with a man who was old enough to be her father. Toni's father had sent her a letter full of Bible verses, underlined in red, about adultery and the wrath of God it brought upon those who dared to go that way.

"What business did you have writing to my father, you fool? Is he the one who chose you for me in the first place?" Toni had shouted at Edgar.

Edgar had gone into a rage, tearing up her collection of poems and calling her a whore. Toni had, in response, grabbed the photo of their wedding, that hung in their living room and smashed it against the wall, the glass shattering into tiny pieces.

Toni wanted to move out and rent her own place, but she couldn't. Her brother Ken, was due to arrive in a few weeks. Ken wanted to study fine art, as he'd always wished, but their father was against it; he didn't think being an artist was a good career choice. Toni had spent hours on the phone with her father, trying to persuade him to let Ken study art in Nairobi.

"Have you seen how poor African artists are? My son is not going to walk around in dreadlocks, claiming to be an artist, while living at home with his parents until he's an old man." Toni's father had been adamant.

"Why don't you send him to France then? He can live with me and go to an art school here," she had suggested, at least as compromise.

"I'll think about it," her father had replied.

Ken landed in France in the summer of 1999, right when Toni and Edgar were fighting and their marriage breaking up. He enrolled at the Alliance Française, to learn French. He could not apply to an art school before he could speak French. He moved into their flat at La Reynerie. Since they only had two-bedrooms, Toni had to move back to the main bedroom and share a bed with her husband.

George was happy to give Ken a job at Le Bagamoyo. The chef was leaving to pursue his studies in another town. In his place, Edgar had been promoted to chef. Ken took Edgar's post as the dish washer. Every evening, Edgar and Ken left for work together, which left Toni free to see Jean-Pierre. He picked her up after they left, drove her to his house, where they had dinner and then made love, before dropping her back at around midnight.

The boys finished work at 2.00am. They often went out for a drink with colleagues. After six months, Ken felt he was ready to rent his own flat, so he moved out, leaving Toni and Edgar alone.

Toni decided to move out of the flat. Jean-Pierre had already proposed that she move into his house, but that would be like officially accepting that she was his girlfriend. Besides, Edgar could have also used it against her in a court of law, because they weren't legally divorced.

Her job at Ma Première Page would enable her to take care of her living expenses, which were minimal. She found a room in a large apartment, which had a bed and a chair. She would have to share the bathroom with her new landlord and his son, but that didn't bother her; anything to move out of that house which had become a source of distress for her. The cold war and endless arguments with Edgar had gone too far.

One evening while Edgar was working, she put all her clothes and books in a suitcase and left. Jean-Pierre drove her to her new flat, where she deposited her huge suitcase then left with him, to his house. For the two months that she rented the room, Toni never once spent a night in it. That was her official address, but she lived with Jean-Pierre, Isabelle and Léo.

Jean-Pierre encouraged Toni not to give up on getting a driving licence. He found her another school and enrolled her in it. He paid the fee and helped Toni revise at home, with extra DVDs and questions. Toni finally passed the Driving Code test. She could now start the driving lessons.

Learning how to drive was a daunting task for Toni, who was very poor at coordinating her movements. She took so many hours of driving, that her driving instructor, Loic, became a friend. Toni failed her first driving test and was so disappointed, she decided to give up altogether, but Jean-Pierre wouldn't let her.

"I'll teach you how to drive properly. You have to get your licence because I want to buy you a car," he insisted. Jean-Pierre let Toni drive one of his three cars, on Sundays, at the parking of the supermarket because it was empty. Toni started gaining confidence and was ready to take the test again. But she failed a second time!

For the next few weeks, she watched other drivers' whizz by on the road as she walked on the sidewalk, wondering what they had that she didn't have.

Loic was equally disappointed and couldn't understand why Toni had failed again.

"Toni, you're a university graduate, for heaven's sake! I know so many people who can't read or write who passed their driving test on the first try. What's wrong with you?"

Loic's words hurt Toni, but he was right, she thought. What was wrong with her?

Toni met Jessica in the Metro. "Hey, are you Kenyan?" Toni asked the plump, dark-skinned girl who was sitting opposite her.

Jessica was startled to hear somebody speaking English.

"Yes, I am. How did you guess?" Jessica asked.

"From your bracelet."

Jessica was wearing a typical Maasai bracelet. The two Kenyan girls were thrilled; it was like meeting a long-lost sister. They discovered that they had many friends in common, from high school and university back in Kenya. Jessica had studied at the University of Nairobi in the same years Toni had gone to Kenyatta University. In Toulouse, she was a student at the Catholic Institute.

She lived alone in a small flat in the St Cyprien area, and worked as a babysitter for a rich family. Jessica loved to dance and every weekend she went out to discotheques with her classmates.

“Come on Toni! Let’s go out this weekend!” She would often say. Toni really wanted to go out and have fun with her agemates, but Jean-Pierre had become very attached to her and sulked anytime she suggested going to spend a night in the room she rented. He gladly gave her money for the rent and spoiled her silly with new clothes, shoes, and lingerie, but he’d begun to act as if Toni were his personal property or a handbag that had to be close to him all the time. It was beginning to irritate Toni.

It is for this reason that Toni went to her rented room when Jean-Pierre was at work. Jessica came with her because she didn’t have class that day. Toni opened the door with the key her new landlord had handed her the day she had signed the lease. The house was quiet, so they thought the landlord and his son were out. Toni’s room was upstairs. As they were walking up the stairs, the landlord suddenly emerged from one of the rooms, making the girls jump with fright.

“Sorry, I was in the dark room,” he said cheerfully. “I have to develop these photos by tomorrow morning.”

He had explained that he was a professional photographer, but Toni didn’t know he had a dark room in the house. In fact, she didn’t know much about him because she only went to the house to pick up clothes when she needed to.

“Would you like me to take a photo of you?” he asked. “For free, of course,” he added.

Toni and Jessica agreed, mainly out of curiosity and because they had the time. He instructed them to sit on the large, leather sofa on one end of the room before he started clicking his camera away.

"Excellent! Perfect! Fantastic! Beautiful!" he exclaimed as he clicked away. He went on and on and within a few minutes, he had them puffed up with the confidence of runway models.

"Now, remove your jackets and let's try out some new poses." The girls obliged, enjoying this new role.

Half an hour later, Toni and Jessica stood there, looking at each other wondering, how and why they had taken off all their clothes.

Suddenly, they both had a feeling that they'd been victims of a ruse or some kind of hypnosis. It finally struck them that they'd just taken nude shots.

"How can you just undress and pose for photos with a man you don't know?" Jean-Pierre growled when Toni mentioned the incident a few days later.

"You are so naïve. What if he had raped you?"

"But how could he rape two girls?" Toni reasoned.

"What if he had a gun?" Jean-Pierre pursued. "He could have tied you up and raped you Toni!"

After that incident, Toni got scared of the landlord and cancelled her lease. She persuaded Jessica to leave her flat, and together they rented a bigger flat. Jean-Pierre agreed to be their guarantor. He went a notch better and paid the rent deposit for them. The main furniture – the beds, chairs, and tables – came with the flat but the girls had to buy a TV, a microwave, and a few other necessities.

Jean-Pierre paid for all these without a complaint. As long as Toni spent every night in his house, he didn't mind spending money on her flat or her friends.

Chapter TEN

Three months into their relationship, Jean-Pierre introduced Toni to Bernadette, his elder sister. Bernadette was fifty-five and held a senior position at the Credit Lyonnais Bank. She was married to Daniel, a typical French man who complained about everything from sunrise to sunset. They had a son, Louis, who was very close to his cousin, Léo.

Bernadette was a beautiful woman, with blonde shoulder-length hair and big blue eyes that seemed to glint every time she smiled. Her nails were always painted red and Toni never once saw her without make-up.

Toni didn't know how tall she was because she was paralysed in her lower limbs and was condemned to using a wheelchair for the rest of her life. Jean-Pierre had informed Toni that his sister had contracted polio as a child and had never walked a single day in her life. The wheelchair was hardly an obstacle for her; she cheerfully went about her household duties like any other person. She would mop, hoover, and dust from her wheelchair. Her house had been built to suit her condition; wider corridors and doors allowed her free movement.

Jean-Pierre often invited Bernadette and her family over for lunch, but the meal would almost always turn into an argument about Isabelle. Bernadette felt that Jean-Pierre was too hard on his children, especially Isabelle. Jean-Pierre felt that Bernadette, who was very close to her niece, was encouraging his daughter to be "a lazy bum like her mother." Toni was shocked that Jean-Pierre could talk ill of his late wife, and with such ease. It wasn't the first time he had said bad things about Isabelle's mum. One day, during an argument with Isabelle, he had raised his hand, almost hitting her.

"You want to hit me the way you used to hit mum?" Isabelle had screamed.

"You deserve it, just the way she did because you have the same sharp tongue!" Jean-Pierre had shouted back but had not touched Isabelle.

Toni and Bernadette slowly became good friends and would sometimes go shopping together, or for coffee. Bernadette told Toni that their parents had disowned Jean-Pierre when he started dating a black woman, Isabelle's late mother.

Six months into Toni and Jean Pierre's relationship, Isabelle ran away from home. She packed her things, took her son with her, and ran off to live with her gypsy boyfriend in his caravan. It was all downhill from there. Jean-Pierre was outraged and threatened to shoot the man who was ruining his daughter's life and raze down the caravan. He drank more in the subsequent months. He would end up in a drunken stupor, slumbered like a log on the sofa every evening.

He tried to go after Isabelle's boyfriend, but the two lovebirds had anticipated his reaction and moved the caravan to an unknown location. He tried his police and detective skills to bring Isabelle back home in vain. She never called or showed any sign of life. It was driving Jean-Pierre crazy. He turned into a moody, angry alcoholic.

In the midst of all this alcohol-induced madness that was swallowing up her brother, Bernadette phoned Toni.

"I have something to tell you, but you must promise never to tell Jean-Pierre," she said.

Bernadette knew where Isabelle was hiding. She revealed that Isabelle hadn't run away because of her fights with her father, as they had assumed. She had taken off because she was expecting a second child. She knew that her father would kill her if he found out, so she had preferred to run away. Bernadette had only found out because Isabelle had reached out to her for some cash. Toni vowed never to tell Jean-Pierre, but she felt bad about having to keep this from him. He was losing his mind over his daughter, drinking himself silly and unleashing his anger and frustrations on Toni. She confided in Bernadette, who advised her to leave Jean-Pierre.

"My brother is not a stable man, Toni. You're a young girl with a bright future ahead of you. Leave him before he hurts you badly," she insisted.

The note of urgency in Bernadette's voice scared Toni, but she did not know how to leave Jean-Pierre, who had practically taken over her life. He was so possessive and jealous that he couldn't stand a single minute of Toni's absence from him, except when they had to go to work. He would wait for her every day at the school, ready to whisk her away with him, not even allowing her a minute of interaction with her colleagues.

Toni nearly choked on Jean-Pierre's constant presence around her and could no longer spend even one night with Jessica at the flat or go out dancing with her friends. She wondered if it was really love or some sort of manic obsession. He would shower her with gifts, pay all her bills, throw lavish parties at his house, and invite her brother and her friends, cook exquisite French dishes and buy all sorts of expensive drinks to entertain them, but he wouldn't allow her even one evening out with them, without him.

Toni was embarrassed to be seen with him in public, so she preferred to stay home than go out with him. Sometimes, after begging and pleading, he would let her out for an evening. If they went out to a restaurant, he would demand to know the name of the restaurant. Her phone would ring incessantly, disrupting the meal and ruining the evening for Toni and her friends. If she switched off her phone or wouldn't answer his calls for any reason, he would call Jessica. If Jessica refused to pick his calls, he would call the restaurant and demand to speak to her. This badgering and nagging would go on the whole night. Sometimes he would drive all the way in the middle of the night and bang on the door until they let him in and wouldn't leave the house without her. Toni had become a prisoner of passion.

On a random afternoon in August, when the Toulouse summer heat was at its peak, Jean-Pierre invited his friends, Bertrand and Alice, for the weekend. Toni had met the couple before; she found them boring and dull, so she invited

Jessica over to keep her company. She would have preferred to be at her flat with Jessica, watching movies and chatting in Swahili, but Jean-Pierre wouldn't have let her go.

Lunch was Jean-Pierre's famous "Boeuf Bourgignon," washed down with copious amounts of red wine. When the meal was over, Toni, Jessica and Alice cleared the table as the men drank their coffee.

"What shall we do this afternoon, Chérie?", Jean-Pierre asked casually as Toni was walking across the room from the kitchen towards the dining room holding a wet sponge in her hand, ready to wipe the table clean of bread crumbs and food.

"I don't know," Toni shrugged in response without looking at him.

Before she could say another word, Jean-Pierre had sprung to his feet and charged towards her. He grabbed Toni by the shoulders and slammed her on the floor.

"Jean-Pierre, stop it!" Jessica gasped and screamed.

Jean-Pierre had his foot on Toni's neck and was hurling insults and all manner of expletives at her.

"You dirty little prostitute!" he barked. "What don't you know? I'll kill you!" he snarled at a dazed Toni.

Jean-Pierre then reached into his front pocket and pulled out a 200-Franc note. It was the year 2000 and Europe was yet to transition to the Euro. He grabbed Toni's chin with one hand and forced his fat fingers into her mouth, wrenching it open as she gasped for air.

Jessica was crying and begging Jean-Pierre to stop the madness, but Jean-Pierre's friends watched the spectacle without saying a word or interfering. Jean-Pierre thrust the note into Toni's mouth and shoved it in, willing her to swallow it. The note grazed Toni's throat and hurt so much that she could not even produce a sound. His foot was stepping on her neck and her eyes began to bulge out.

Jean-Pierre suddenly released Toni's neck, straightened his back, and turned towards Jessica, who had been pulling his shirt, to try and stop him. Toni grabbed the chance, jumped to her feet, and ran outside like a gazelle that had just escaped from a lion's grip. She pulled the note out of her throat as she ran, before throwing it on the ground. As she ran towards the gate, Toni shouted at Jessica in Swahili.

"Jessica, *chukua* passport *yangu tafadhali*!" Please take my passport! Jean-Pierre didn't understand Swahili, but he managed to pick out the word "Passport." He yelled back at her, "You can forget about your passport, you dirty little dog. Get out of my house!" he screamed at her.

But Toni was out of the gate by then and only heard the words "You can forget about your passport." As she trotted on the gravel, Toni felt like she was walking on hot coal. She hadn't thought about her shoes when she ran out. She was barefoot.

She walked in the direction of Toulouse, crying hysterically, wiping the mucous from her runny nose on her blouse. There was no public transportation in Lespinasse on Sundays and even if there had been, she didn't have a single cent on her. Suddenly she remembered the 200-Franc note she had extracted from her throat. The coppery taste returned to her taste buds with a newness that felt as if the note was still in her mouth.

Just then a car came up behind her and slowed down. She hoped the driver wouldn't notice her sorry state; she didn't want to encounter any offers for help because she did not want to answer any questions. She just wanted to keep on walking, away from Jean-Pierre, and at the same time hoping that he wouldn't harm Jessica who'd tried to rescue her. The car stopped on her left, about three metres in front of her. Toni had her eyes fixed on the ground as she walked, replaying the horrible experience she had just been through and wondering how she was going to get herself out of the mess that was her relationship with Jean Pierre. The car's door suddenly opened and to her horror, Toni realized with a chill that it was Jean-Pierre. Before she could take off, Jean-Pierre had stepped out of the car and grabbed her by the arm.

"Where the hell do you think you are going?" he cursed, as he opened the passenger door and threw Toni inside like a piece of luggage.

He slammed the door and activated the central lock. He went around the car, used the key to open the driver's door, and rolled into the driver's seat. He banged shut his own door and without uttering a word, turned the ignition and stepped on the accelerator with all his might.

"We're dying today, the two of us together," he pronounced as the car jerked forward, nearly sending Toni out through the windscreen.

Toni felt her back go cold, at the chilling announcement.

"I know you've been planning to leave me. I can't let you do that. I love you too much. I'd rather kill you and kill myself than let you go. No other man will have you if I can't. You're mine Toni, do you understand? Mine alone!"

Toni's primordial instincts checked in and adrenaline began to course through her veins. Something about the way he spoke filled her with morbid fear. Jean-Pierre had completely lost it.

"I love you Jean-Pierre," Toni began. "I will never leave you," she added, trembling.

Jean-Pierre drove on, with a grim look, not heeding to her pleas.

"Let's go back to the house J-P. I have a secret to tell you," Toni tried some more. It was her only chance and she took it.

"I know where Isabelle is," Toni blurted out, the words gushing out of her mouth in panic. This time Jean-Pierre heard her and responded with a slamming of the brakes.

What had she just done? Toni wondered but recovered quickly and composed herself. It did not matter, Toni argued inwardly, if she had to betray both Bernadette and Isabelle, she would. After all, it was a matter of life and death. She either kept the secret or saved her life. She chose her life.

Jean-Pierre turned the car around and raced towards the house with renewed vigour as if he was a rally driver who had been in the lead and had taken a wrong turn and was now rushing back to the correct route.

When they got to his house, he led Toni straight to his bedroom, walking past his friends and Jessica as if they were not there. They sat down on the bed. Toni recounted what Bernadette had confided in her. Jean-Pierre suddenly grabbed her and kissed her hard on her mouth, hurting her slightly. His tongue roughly parted her lips and plunged in. He launched into nibbling on her lower lip with his teeth.

"You're hurting me Jean-Pierre," she pleaded.

But his hands were all over her body, kneading her as if she were some pizza dough. The same man who had tried to murder her barely an hour earlier, calling her "dirty little dog," was now peeling off every piece of clothing from her body. Toni was confused. Was this love or hate?

Jean-Pierre sprang to his feet, kicked the door shut and took off all his clothes. This time, instead of roughing her up, he licked her pussy ever so gently, caressing her thighs softly, and planting little warm kisses all over her body. Toni was there physically, but her mind was far away, even as Jean-Pierre spread her thighs and buried his head between them. She wanted him to stop, but she was scared. He was now inside her, thrusting and breathing heavily.

He was so ugly, she thought. He reminded her of a pig; a filthy old pig. She hated him. She wanted to throw up. Jean-Pierre suddenly stopped and pulled out of her. That's when Toni noticed that he had been crying.

"I'm so sorry my sweetie," he said as he struggled to hold back tears. "If only you knew how much I love you. I can't live without you, please don't leave me, ever, okay?"

Toni didn't utter a word, she just stared at him blankly. When Toni finally pried herself from his embrace, she noticed his shrivelled penis, lying there like a deflated balloon and wanted to vomit at the sight.

When Bernadette learnt of Toni's betrayal, she was so livid she could not accept any explanation.

"You deserve each other! I hope he beats you up thoroughly, the way he used to beat his wife."

Life with Jean-Pierre had become unbearable, and Toni

felt powerless. She wanted to stop going to Jean-Pierre's, but he stuck to her like a leech. One incident made her want to leave even more.

Toni had never been alone in Jean-Pierre's house. As it happened, she was off-duty as was Jean-Pierre. Then a call came in from Jean-Pierre's office and he had to rush out. Léo was in school and Isabelle had refused to come back home, even after Jean-Pierre traced her to her hideout. Jean-Pierre had left the dogs outside, but in his rush, he had forgotten to leave them drinking water. The dogs started barking. Toni took a jug, filled it with water and went outside to refill their bowls.

On her way back into the house, Toni found Hugo, the male dog, standing in her path, gritting his teeth, and snarling at her. Toni stopped, terror all over her that she was sure her blood froze. Hugo growled some more, a deep, frightening growl. Toni stayed rooted to the spot. In the blink of an eye, Hugo jumped on Toni, whose piercing scream rent the air as she tumbled to the ground. In that instant, Olympe, the female dog, dashed across the compound, barking at both woman and dog as if she was going to join in the attack. Then the strangest thing happened: Olympe began to fight off Hugo as if trying to stop him from attacking Toni. She took Hugo's paw in her mouth and began pulling him away.

Toni was terrified, and her voice had become hoarse from screaming. A man walking down the street saw the commotion and ran towards the gate, shouting at the top of his voice. As soon as Hugo heard the stranger's voice, he turned around and charged at the gate, barking and baring his enormous yellow teeth, with Olympe in tow. Hugo could not go over the gate or fence, but the man did not wait to find out. He ran across the road and was nearly knocked down by a car that came to a screeching halt. Toni fled back into the house, slammed the door shut and engaged all the locks before throwing herself on the couch, sobbing.

Everything Jean-Pierre did grated on Toni's nerves. Even his kind gestures and gifts annoyed her. One Saturday afternoon after they'd had lunch, Jean-Pierre pulled out a bottle of Jack Daniels for himself and a bottle of Malibu for Toni. Léo had already disappeared into his room to play video games. Barely an hour later, Jean-Pierre had emptied the bottle of whisky and now sat awkwardly on one of the couches, constantly begging Toni to go lie down with him. Toni waved away the requests and continued reading the Douglas Kennedy novel she had picked up from the bookshop earlier that week as she took small sips of the Malibu. Jean-Pierre blacked out a few minutes later. Toni looked at him with a tinge of pity. It seemed like the right time to pry herself from his hold and just start over a new life. The thought fired her up and soon she was calling Jessica.

"I am leaving this man Jessica, I've had it," Toni wailed into the handset in Swahili, her voice sombre and on the verge of a sob.

"Toni, what happened this time?" Jessica nearly screamed back in dread.

"Nothing happened, I'm okay. But I can't do this anymore, Jessica. He's here lying on the couch, completely drunk. He has gone bonkers and he will surely sink into madness soon. I don't want to wait around for it," Toni explained.

"Toni, you keep saying you're leaving. But you never do. I don't know what to tell you.", Jessica said sadly.

Jessica often wondered how Toni could draw even an ounce of joy or happiness from what she considered a very toxic relationship. What made Toni stay even after all the fights and threats?

"Who are you talking to?" Jean-Pierre's voice broke out before Toni turned around to see him stagger towards her.

"No one, I mean, it's just Jessica ..." she answered, her voice quavering.

Before she could utter another word, Jean-Pierre grabbed the handset and slammed it on the floor.

"What are you talking about? Are you planning to leave me?" he asked, a note of warning creeping into his voice.

Jean-Pierre grabbed Toni and slammed her on the couch with so much force it moved back about an inch. Her silence made him angrier because it seemed to be a confirmation that she intended to leave. With Toni still on her back on the sofa, Jean-Pierre left and went to his bedroom. Toni stood up, wondering what to do. She couldn't run away like the last time; he would just come after her.

Then Jean-Pierre came back into the room, a revolver in his hand. He grabbed Toni and pressed the gun against her temple.

Toni froze as soon the metal touched the skin of her forehead. She screamed before he placed his hand over her mouth.

"Shut up!" he ordered.

"Léo! Come here right now," Jean-Pierre yelled out

across the room.

"Yeah?" asked Léo, as he walked into the room.

Léo froze when he saw his father holding a gun against Toni's head, staring in horror, with his mouth open.

"Come here, right here," Jean-Pierre motioned with his revolver while his other hand gripped Toni's collar. Léo reluctantly obeyed, making slow heavy steps towards them.

"Look at her for the last time and say your goodbyes. She is going to die right now!" Jean-Pierre pronounced. Tears rolled down Léo's cheeks as he covered his mouth with both hands.

"Didn't you hear me? Say it! Tell her goodbye!" Jean-Pierre ordered.

Léo shook his head in a slow side to side motion. "No papa. Don't do it. Don't kill her. Just forgive her," Léo finally managed, his words mixed up with sobs.

"Get the hell out of here," Jean-Pierre barked. Léo fled the scene, went back to his bedroom, and locked the door.

"Please don't kill me Jean-Pierre," Toni pleaded. "I will never leave you. I promise."

A memory suddenly flashed in front of her. It was vivid, as if it had happened just the week before. She saw the police carry Musa's body out of his house, in a body bag. She heard the screams and the songs as his relatives learnt of his death. She saw the women sobbing. Toni then heard her father say, "Her headmaster is no more."

Tears started flowing freely from her eyes. She was going to die. Jean-Pierre was going to shoot her. What would her parents do?

How would her body be transported back to Nairobi? She wished she had left Jean-Pierre the day he had stuffed the 200-franc note down her throat. Or the day he had shoved her out of his moving car. Luckily, he hadn't been driving fast and she had only got a few scratches on her elbows, as she fell on the kerb.

"Why did you want to leave me Toni? I'll kill you and kill myself. We will both die, you hear me? I told you I can't live without you. If I can't have you, no other man will!" Jean-Pierre threatened, as he pressed the barrel of the gun on different parts of Toni's head.

Dark thoughts about the end of her life filled up Toni's mind. Nausea assailed her. When she next opened her mouth to speak, Toni threw up with so much force that her vomit splashed against Jean-Pierre's chest, who in a moment of panic, suddenly dropped her and stood back.

"*Putain de merde!*" "Shit! Shit! Shit!", Jean-Pierre cursed as he took two steps backwards.

Toni proceeded to vomit on the floor, only stopping to catch her breath. Jean-Pierre walked back to his room and put the gun away.

He came back with a bucket and mop and cleaned the mess Toni had made. Jessica had listened in on the entire altercation over the phone, whose receiver Jean-Pierre had slammed to the floor without disconnecting. She did not see the gun pressed at Toni's temple!

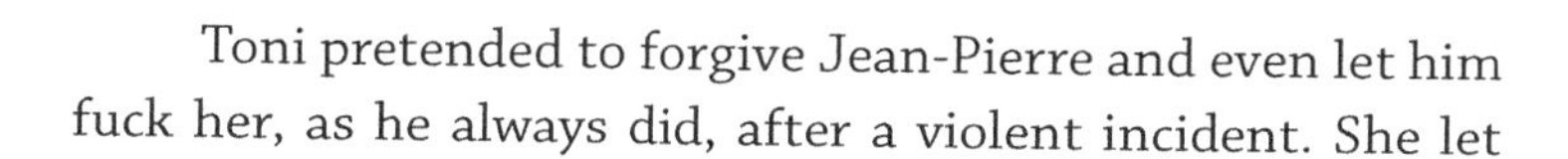

Toni pretended to forgive Jean-Pierre and even let him fuck her, as he always did, after a violent incident. She let him undress her and caress her. She did not complain when he licked her pussy. And when he penetrated her, she opened her legs wide and let him thrust and empty himself into her, without a word. When he finally released her, and he was snoring away, she went to the bathroom and ran herself a hot bath. She scrubbed herself so hard, she thought she would bleed. She was scrubbing Jean-Pierre out of her life.

She had made up her mind. This was the curtain call; there would be no more plays. The show was over.

The following morning, Jean-Pierre dropped Toni off at work as usual. As soon as she entered the school, she ran to Nathalie's office. Toni had been working at the school for over a year, and she had forged a close friendship with her boss.

"Nathalie, you have to change my shift or my working hours, please," Toni breathed out the words.

"This man will kill me."

Nathalie was aware of her situation because Toni often confided in her. "Ok, you can leave two hours earlier," Nathalie offered.

Toni was relieved that Jean-Pierre would not find her at the school when he came to pick her up in the evening. When she left that evening, Toni ran as fast as she could to the Metro. Everyone walking in front of her on the street seemed to be on slow motion, and even the Metro seemed to have reduced its speed. She arrived at the apartment and let herself in since Jessica was not at home.

"Toni, I've been waiting out here for ten minutes. Where are you?" Jean-Pierre began when Toni answered her phone. "It is ...."

"Jean-Pierre," Toni cut him short. "It is over between you and me. I am never coming back to your house. Forget me. I'm going to hang up now."

Then the line went dead.

Jean-Pierre dropped his cellphone on the passenger seat, got out of the car, and went inside the school in search of Toni. Nathalie was shocked to see a huge, panting man at the door when she answered the bell.

"Where's Toni?" he asked in his booming voice, which would scare the little children if he stayed one more minute.

"Toni is on leave for two weeks," Nathalie lied.

She wanted to make sure he never came back to the school. He stormed out, cursing under his breath. He got into his car and reversed dangerously, almost running over a cyclist.

In the weeks that followed the break-up, Jean-Pierre kept calling Toni and many of her friends. He would tell Toni's friends all the unpalatable things Toni had ever said about them.

"She thinks you're ugly and that your boyfriend stinks," he told one of her friends.

"Your wife is cheating on you with your friend," he told a husband of one of Toni's friends.

Because of his job, he had access to everybody's phone number and address and didn't hesitate to look up all her friends. He also called to issue all manner of threats and to remind her that he was a police commander with a lot of influence in Toulouse.

"I'll have you and your stupid African friends shipped back to your big village!" he'd threaten. "You're all whores and users! After all I did for you, you'll know who I am."

By the time Jean-Pierre was done calling and threatening her friends, Toni had lost almost all of them, except Jessica. The other girls had simply stopped talking to her, after Jean Pierre's revelations. As much as it wasn't her fault, Toni understood their reaction and accepted her fate gracefully.

But Jean-Pierre could only threaten and insult her so much. Gradually, her fears dissipated and as a new resolve engulfed her, she realized that she could not keep running forever. No man was invulnerable. It was time to stand up to Jean-Pierre. Suddenly it occurred to her that she could use his vulnerabilities against him.

"Listen here Jean-Pierre," she began the next time he called, "You might have me deported back to Africa, but at least I'll be going back home, to my parents. I didn't fall off a tree, you know. As for you, once I'm done reporting that your daughter once stole your gun and that she takes drugs, we'll see who'll be in more hot soup," she paused.

"And remember the bar on rue de Belfort that you and your police friends go to? You think I don't know that it's full of people sniffing coke and prostitutes - and that you drink for free in exchange for turning a blind eye to drug trafficking," Toni's voice trailed off.

After that conversation, Jean-Pierre backed off. But not before asking Toni to return everything he had ever bought her and her friends. The flat was nearly empty when he finally came to pick up all his stuff.

"I can't believe we never even bought ourselves a microwave; a bloody microwave," Jessica sighed as she sat on the old, sagging couch, the one that had come with the flat.

Jean-Pierre had gifted them a new IKEA sofa, but now he had taken it back. The girls had heaved all the stuff and left it downstairs, so that Jean-Pierre wouldn't have to come into the apartment. For some strange reason, Toni no longer feared Jean-Pierre. In fact, she seemed to spoil for a fight.

"Do you also want the panties? The lingerie?" She asked Jean-Pierre, when he came to pick up his things.

Jean-Pierre never bothered Toni again.

Chapter ELEVEN

In 2000, Edgar left France for good. He had never liked France; if anything, he had only come because of Toni. Now that their marriage was over, he had no reason to continue cooking chicken and meat balls at Le Bagamoyo. He applied for a school in the USA and said *au revoir* to the Pink City.

Ken, Toni's brother, had joined an art school and was immersed in living his childhood dream. He had quickly found his footing in Toulouse and made friends. Toni saw him on some weekends, because he still worked at Le Bagamoyo in the evenings, but only on weekends. Jessica had also started working at Le Bagamoyo as a waitress.

With Edgar gone, and Jean-Pierre off her back, Toni was happy to hang out at the restaurant. Sometimes she helped, when there were too many customers. Toni and Jessica still lived in the small flat up in the attic with the slanted walls. When they weren't working in the evening, they'd throw parties and invite their friends, mostly young men they met in pubs or at Le Bagamoyo.

It is in one of these parties that she met Michel, who had been invited by Jules, one of their friends.

"Hi Toni, meet Michel," Jules said, when Toni opened the door. Michel was a tall, blue-eyed guy in his thirties. He had to bend really low to enter the flat and couldn't stay upright without banging his head on the roof. As all the other guests danced, he had to sit on the worn-out sofa, drinking beer. The round table in the middle of the room was filled with bottles; some full, some empty. There were wine bottles, beers, vodka, soda and a few plastic tumblers, strewn about. The ashtray was overflowing and some of the ash had poured on the red tablecloth.

"Toni, would you like to go to the club with me?" Michel asked. "I'd like to dance, but your flat will break my neck," he joked.

"I'll come with you," Jules chimed in.

Toni looked around for Jessica, but she wasn't among the couples dancing in the living room. Maybe she'd disappeared into her bedroom with the guy she'd been kissing. Jules and Toni got into Michel's car, a small Renault 5 that had seen better days. Before taking off, Michel had reached into his glove compartment and taken out a tin. He then rolled himself a cigarette.

After he'd fastened his seat belt, he planted the cigarette between his lips and with a lighter, lit up one of its ends. He rolled down his window with one hand, engaged the first gear and the car began moving. The wind blew some of the smoke to the back of the car as they drove off. An unfamiliar smell filled the car. It was not the usual cigarette smell. After a few puffs, Michel passed it to Jules, who in turn, rolled down his window and pulled hard on the cigarette. It finally dawned on Toni. It was not a cigarette, but marijuana. Jules turned around and made a gesture as if to pass the joint to her.

"No thanks, I don't smoke joints," Toni declined politely.

The club was packed when they arrived, but they managed to find a table by the wall. Michel sat next to Toni on the bench-like sofa.

"What would you guys like to drink?" Jules asked.

"I'll have a glass of white wine," Toni returned excitedly.

"Toni," Michel jumped in. "Nightclubs do not sell glasses of wine. Get a bottle Jules, we'll share". Toni felt embarrassed; she had never been to a nightclub before.

"Would you like to dance?" Michel asked.

The DJ was playing *"Sexual healing"* by Marvin Gaye. Michel put his hands around Toni's waist and moved with her to the beat of the music. He was so tall that Toni had to stand on her toes like a ballet dancer, as she tried to put her hands around his neck. She felt as if he was carrying her around rather than dancing with her. When the song ended, Toni expected them to go back to their table, but Michel surprised her by keeping his hands around her waist and kissing her on the lips. Something about the way he suddenly kissed her reminded her of John Mark and a deserted alley in Nairobi.

Michel dropped Toni back to her flat, with a promise to pick her up the next day.

Michel lived alone in a studio flat, not far from Ma Première Page. It was a typical bachelor's flat: a big room with a kitchenette in a corner; a two-stove cooker and a small fridge. The main room contained a double bed, a chair, and a table that held DJ material. On a shelf was a huge collection of old LPs.

"I'm a social worker at the Toulouse town hall, but I hate my job," Michel said to Toni when they got talking later. "My passion is music. I volunteer as a DJ for a local radio, 'Radio Campus'. My brother and I host a Jazz programme every Thursday night," he added.

The only available place for one to sit was on the bed. When Michel picked up Toni at lunchtime, they passed by McDonald's and bought takeaway lunch. Toni could hear Jean-Pierre's voice saying "McDonald's is shit food" in her head as she bit into her burger, savouring its taste. Michel had put on some soft Jazz music.

When they finished eating, they lay on the bed and talked about themselves. Toni told him about her failed marriage and her crazy relationship with the mad cop. He told her how he had lived for two years with a girl, before she left him for another guy.

Michel started running his long fingers up Toni's arm. Toni had put on her little red dress that had laces at the front like a shoe. She had bought it at the flea market of La Reynerie, when she was still married to Edgar. Michel started undoing the laces, slowly. Toni felt awkward. What was she supposed to do? Caress his hair? The laces undone, Michel lifted the little red dress over Toni's head and hung it on the chair. He cupped her head in his hands and placed his lips on hers, as Freddie Jackson's "That's all I'll ever ask" played in the background. Michel kissed Toni to the rhythm of the music, making her feel like she was drifting away into the music. His hands went down to caress her inner thighs gently, as if with a feather, as his soft lips mingled with hers.

Making love to sweet jazz music was a first for Toni. It was the most heavenly feeling, she thought to herself, as Michel swayed his hips to the rhythm of the music.

"You're beautiful. Your skin is like silk," he whispered into Toni's ear.

Going to work from Michel's house was more convenient than taking the Metro from her flat, so Toni started spending more nights at Michel's.

Jessica was a bit worried.

"Toni, you're never at home. It feels like the days you were with Jean-Pierre. Are you sure you're not moving too fast?"

"Relax. Michel is not like Jean-Pierre. He's a cool guy," Toni would defend herself.

Michel had a lot of friends who often threw parties in their flats. Toni was easily accepted into their group, but she didn't quite fit in. Most of them were former schoolmates of Michel's. Toni didn't have any tales or reminisces to share with them. They smoked a lot of marijuana and passed the joints around. Not one to be left out for long, Toni decided to try a joint one day.

"I'm going to take a puff today," Toni declared when a joint was passed around.

Michel was surprised, "Oh really? Fine. Here..."

Toni took a pull at the joint, the way she did when she smoked a cigarette. She passed the joint to Jules and waited for the famous "great" effects she used to hear about. But what happened next was the most uncomfortable feeling she had ever felt: she started burping and hiccupping, her chest felt constricted, she couldn't breathe.

"Michel, I can't breathe", she panted.

"Ha! Ha! Ha! That's because you don't know how to inhale properly. Just relax, it will pass," Michel laughed, as he pulled on the joint.

Toni was so uncomfortable that she had to go and lay down on a bed and wait for the burps and hiccups to subside. This took three hours. She vowed never to touch another joint in her life.

"I'm tired of paying rent for a flat I never sleep in. We should take a flat together. Jessica would like to move in with her boyfriend, anyway." Toni said to Michel.

"We've only been together three months; I think it's too early," Michel replied.

Toni decided to spend more nights at her flat with Jessica. But Michel had grown fond of her company but didn't like spending nights in her flat. He gave in and agreed to take a flat with her. They got a big, airy, three-bedroomed flat at La Roseraie, a walking distance from Ma Première Page. It had wide French windows and a big balcony.

Toni had insisted on a three-bedroomed flat because she wanted to have a room for her shoes and clothes, and a room for Michel's DJ equipment. Michel was happy to have a big flat with a balcony, but for a different reason. He started growing marijuana in a cupboard, complete with a watering and lighting system. He also grew weed on the balcony, which stressed Toni because it was illegal.

"What if the police spot it Michel? We could get arrested!" she protested.

"They can't see it; we're on the fourth floor; you can't tell what plant it is from the ground," he tried to convince her.

When he wasn't in his music room trying out mixes with his headphones on, Michel was busy tending to his plants; pruning, wiping, watering.... for hours.

Michel was also very close to his mother, who didn't live very far. Every Sunday, they would go over to his parents for lunch. They had to be there at exactly noon because his father was diabetic and had to eat at fixed times. Toni liked dancing and staying out every Saturday, until the wee hours, at Le Bagamoyo, but hated having to wake up early on Sunday and prepare for this ritual.

When Michel needed to buy a winter jacket, he would go with his mother to the shop, which amused Toni at the beginning.

One day Michel's mother passed by the house unannounced. She said she was on her way to town and had decided to drop in and check on them.

"I think you should move the fridge to this corner," she suggested, as she looked around the kitchen, opening cupboards and drawers. Toni was taken aback by this strange behaviour but didn't say anything.

"Ok. We'll do that," Michel replied and immediately started moving the fridge to where his mother had suggested.

When Michel's mother finally left and had barely gone down the full flight of stairs, Toni began to move the fridge back to its original position, dragging and pushing it with all her might. Michel returned from seeing off his mother just as Toni was moving the final few inches.

"What are you doing?" he cried. "But mother said that ..."

"Said what?" Toni replied curtly. "Is this her house?" she hissed.

"It is not for your mother to decide where I am going to put my fridge!"

Michel had never encountered this side of Toni and was obviously shocked.

Above all, Michel was addicted to his music. He would spend hours in his DJ room with headphones on, with a huge joint in his mouth, and wouldn't come out of his studio except to go to the bathroom or to eat. Toni would often find herself alone, watching TV, or reading.

"Michel, dinner is ready!" Toni announced cheerfully one evening. Michel was in his studio, as always, preparing for his radio programme. He had his headphones on so he didn't hear, as usual.

Toni walked into his studio and shouted, "Hey, dinner is ready!"

"I'm not hungry! I'll eat later!" he shot back. He was in the middle of an interesting mix and didn't appreciate the interruption.

"You don't love me Michel," Toni shouted in reply. "You love your music and your plants more than you love me," she added, agitated.

Michel had already put his headphones back on and didn't hear Toni, which frustrated her even more.

In a fit of anger, Toni walked to the balcony, grabbed two of his plants and broke the stems, then went back to the kitchen. When Michel went to check on his plants before turning in, he couldn't believe what he saw.

"Toni, why did you break my plants?" he asked. His face had turned red.

"Because you love them more than you love me!" Toni screamed.

Michel grabbed Toni by the shoulders and threw her violently on the sofa, then walked out of the flat.

The relationship went sour very quickly. It was reduced to a series of arguments about Michel and his marijuana, to say nothing of his ever-present mother.

As was customary every Sunday, Michel and Toni had gone to his parents' house for lunch. Earlier in the week, Toni had mentioned to Michel that they needed to buy a new frying pan.

"Look," Michel's mother said, handing Toni a wrapped package, "I bought you a frying pan."

"Why did you buy us a frying pan?" Toni asked, packing all the politeness she could muster in her question.

"Michel said you needed a frying pan."

When they got home that evening, Toni was furious. "I told you we needed to buy a frying pan, I didn't tell you to ask your mother to buy us a frying pan!"

Toni took to spending almost all her evenings at Le Bagamoyo. Michel was too busy with his music to pay her any attention, she had concluded. They now lived together but were not sharing anything other than the bills and the house. They'd turned into roommates. Sex became a rare occurrence because they didn't create time for it. The few times they were together, all they did was argue and fight.

"I don't see why I keep taking the pill. We hardly make love and you don't help me pay for it," Toni declared.

"That's your problem," Michel sneered.

Michel had been away on a work trip to Paris for two weeks. When he returned, he was excited to see Toni, which was rare. He was also in a very romantic mood, which was a nice surprise for Toni. He made love to her the way he had done the first time.

There was hope for their relationship, after all, Toni thought to herself.

She had been unhappy for many months and had begun wondering if they were going to stay together. Toni had forgotten that she was not on contraception. When she missed her period, the last thing on her mind had been pregnancy, but she took a test anyway.

"Chérie, I'm pregnant," she announced to Michel.

They both had stable jobs and there was an extra room in the flat. She knew Michel's family and they considered her part of them. She was sure Michel's mum would be delighted by the news of a forthcoming grandchild, the first one for her.

"There's no way we're keeping the baby!" Michel had crushed her hopes with one sentence.

"What will my mother think? If you think you're going to trap me into marrying you, better think twice! You'll have to get rid of it. Abortion is legal in France and it's even refunded by the Social Security. Just book an appointment with your gynaecologist."

Toni felt like somebody had poured a bucket of ice-cold water on her. It took her a while to digest what Michel had just spat out at her. The following day, Toni went to her doctor and swallowed a pill to get rid of her three-week old pregnancy. She did not say anything to Michel and the subject was never discussed again. But something in Toni had died. She knew it was over between her and Michel, but she didn't tell him. She couldn't understand how a full-grown man couldn't make decisions without consulting his mother. Toni had had enough of it. He could marry his mother, if he wanted. She was going to leave him as soon as she'd figured out how.

Toni bought a small mattress and moved out of the main bedroom. She slept on the floor in the spare room. She stopped going to Michel's parents' place for Sunday lunch and only spoke to Michel when it was necessary. As soon as she was done with work at Ma Première Page, she took the Metro straight to Le Bagamoyo and spent the rest of the evening eating, drinking, dancing, and reminiscing about Africa with the other customers. Le Bagamoyo had become her refuge.

It was Toni's last chance to get her driving licence. If she failed this time, she would have to re-sit the Code exam all over again. All the money she had spent from the beginning would have gone to waste.

"It is now or never," she muttered to herself as she walked into the exam centre.

She had not bothered to inform Michel that she was going to sit for her driving test for the third time. They hardly spoke. Toni took long deep breaths as she sat in the car that would be used to test her driving skills. The passenger door suddenly opened and a stocky woman with a square face and thin eyebrows who held her hair back in an unusually long and neat ponytail entered the car.

"Toni," she stated rather than asked, and then flipped a few pages of Toni's file on her clipboard.

"Yes. That's me," Toni returned.

"Okay, let's go. Let's go down the street and then join the highway," she commanded.

"Stay calm and take it easy," she added.

Toni remembered to wear her seatbelt and control the rearview mirrors before driving out of the parking, the way Loic had taught her. She joined the highway smoothly and began to pick up. A huge delivery truck on the adjacent lane suddenly switched lanes, almost forcing her out of the highway. Toni could not react fast enough, and the testing examiner slammed on the brakes and turned the wheel towards her direction, coming within a hair's breadth of smashing onto the side of the truck. The car came to a halt, but the truck resumed its journey as if nothing had happened.

"Okay. That's enough. Let's go back to the station," the examiner said in a calm voice. Toni drove back to the testing centre dejected and mentally prepared for the outcome.

"Wait here," said the examiner as she got out of the car and walked into the office.

Toni was sure it was over for her. She could not afford to start all over. She would have to rely on public transport all her life. In those days, one would know immediately after the test whether they had passed or not. The system was slightly adjusted later due to the rise in number of cases of testing examiners turning up with bloody noses or black eyes from disgruntled applicants. All applicants would now get an email or a note in their mailbox informing them of the outcome of their tests.

Someone rapped on the window and Toni turned to the sight of a yellow slip handed through the window by her driving examiner.

She could not believe her eyes: Three years, three tests, and three thousand Euros later.

Toni had passed her driving test!

Chapter TWELVE

Many important occurrences in Toni's life, both good and bad, seemed to always happen on Thursdays, including her birth. She had just turned twenty-nine.

She had just obtained her driving licence. She had just had an abortion.

On this Thursday, she met Marco.

Toni was sure her boyfriend, Michel, didn't love her. She was more than certain that he was wasting her time. After spending her evening at Le Bagamoyo, Toni would run out of Le Bagamoyo at a few minutes to midnight and jump into the last Metro out of town.

On this Thursday, Toni completely forgot to check her watch and by the time she did, the last Metro had already left.

"George, *tafadhali*, (please) I've just missed the last Metro, can you drop me home please?" she pleaded.

"No problem," George said.

That was classic George. He was used to dropping the girls home whenever they missed the Metro. But Toni would have to wait until he had closed the restaurant for the night. It meant she would not be home before three in the morning. Luckily, the next day was her off day, so she sat back and ordered more Rosé.

When George was done, he closed the restaurant and, with Toni, entered his white van. The van was always parked on the streets and for that George had been fined more times than Toni could count.

As they were leaving, George took a turn opposite to the one he should have taken now that he was dropping Toni home.

"Where are we going, George?" Toni asked, struggling to keep her eyes open as she was both drunk and sleepy.

"I want to say a quick hello to my friend Marco. This won't take long, I promise," he said.

He parked outside a small building in the middle of town and asked Toni to follow him. Toni made out the words "*Zenith*."

They were standing in front of a big black door, which swung open almost immediately when George rang a bell. A bald, burly, muscular, heavily-tattooed mass of human flesh emerged. He nodded at them without as much as a smile, shook their hands and ushered them in.

"*Bonsoir mon ami* George!" echoed a voice from behind them as they walked in. A bald, medium-height and sprightly figure emerged, gave George a hug and kissed Toni on both cheeks.

"Toni, meet my good friend, Marco."

So, this was the famous Marco she had heard so much about. Ingrid, her friend who worked at a café in town, was always talking about him: Marco this, Marco that, just like Marco, ad infinitum. She said her dream was to work for him. George, too, had often spoken about Marco with a lot of admiration and awe. Everybody seemed to have a lot of respect for this Marco who, Toni had gathered, was the Mafioso of Toulouse. He owned Zenith, one of the most popular discotheques in town and was president of the restaurants and hotels trade union. He was very powerful and had close ties with the mayor, politicians, and all influential businesspeople around. Being Marco's friend opened many doors.

As George was chatting with some friends he had met, Toni found a corner at the end of the bar and perched herself on the bar stool.

"What would you like to drink?" a voice shouted over the noise of the music. Toni turned towards the direction of the voice.

"Oh, hello Marco," Toni smiled. "Some wine please."

"Please serve this young lady a glass of Rosé," he instructed the bartender, as he hopped onto a stool next to her.

"Tell me about yourself. I've never seen you around here," he continued.

Toni was surprised by this display of interest from the Great Marco. After asking her more questions about herself, he went behind the bar and came back with a small writing pad, yanked one of the leaflets and wrote down his number.

"Please call me next week. I'd like to have coffee with you," he said, as he handed her the piece of paper.

Toni took the paper and pushed it into the back pocket of her Jeans. Zouk music, which Toni loved absolutely, was now playing.

As far as she was concerned, George was the best Zouk dancer in town. Toni looked around the room and spotted him chatting with two gentlemen. She walked over to him and asked him to dance with her. He handed his drink to one of the gentlemen and grabbed her by her waist, deftly swaying her gently to the rhythm of "*Alors pourquoi tout a changé*."

"George, your friend just gave me his phone number," Toni whispered into his ear in Swahili. "Should I call him?"

George stopped dancing abruptly, held her back and looked at her in shock.

"Are you serious?" he whispered. "Do you know how many women are dying to have Marco's phone number? You must call him without fail."

"Okay! Okay! I will call the great Marco," she muttered, rolling her eyes.

Toni walked back to her stool and slumped on the counter, nearly soaking a few of her shoulder-length dreadlocks into the half finished glass of wine. She was now quite tipsy and sleepy. Using her arms as a pillow, she closed her eyes and slept. She wasn't sure how long she had slept when she was jolted out of her slumber by a conversation between the two men.

"It's okay George, I'll drop her off. You can leave," Toni heard Marco say. George was already in his coat, heading out of the door.

"Hey, wait," she protested weakly, raising her hand in protest.

"What's going on here?" she asked.

"Don't worry, you're in safe hands," Marco interposed. "I will drop you home," he said, emphasizing the I with a double tap of his chest.

"Yeah, you'll be fine Sweetie, you can trust Marco. I'll see you tomorrow," George confirmed.

Well, at least George was okay with it. Toni knew that George would never expose her to any kind of danger. He kissed her on the cheeks and left.

"Let's go Bébé," Marco said after a while.

Toni would discover later that Marco called every one of his women "Bébé," including his wife and his daughters.

"What am I doing in a stranger's car at six o'clock in the morning?" Toni asked herself in a moment of panic.

Toni had always wanted to eat at "La Bonita." La Bonita was a neat Brazilian restaurant in the centre of Toulouse. A friend had told her they served wild game, just like at the Carnivore back in Nairobi. When Michel proposed going to a restaurant the night before she left for Kenya, Toni asked if they could go to La Bonita.

As she walked home from work, she thought about the evening that lay ahead and about what she was about to do. She had made up her mind: Today was the final day. She was flying out to Kenya the following day, it would be her first visit to her motherland since she had relocated to France. She was looking forward to meeting old friends and relatives; she had missed the familiar sounds of matatus in the city, the taste of *nyama choma*, the grilled meat that was a Kenyan specialty, and the beautiful weather all year round.

Her suitcase was almost ready and this time round, she had vowed to carry less clothes and shoes than the first time. Michel entered the flat just as she was putting the last few items into the suitcase.

"Can we leave now?" Michel called out from the door. "It's almost 7.30pm and I booked a table for 8pm. I'm sure we won't find parking in that place. I don't understand what is so special about La Bonita that you had to insist so much on going there."

Toni walked out of the bedroom, picked up her handbag from the sofa and said, "Let's go."

Even though the street looked nothing like its name, Toni liked its name "La rue des Paquerettes" (the street of Daisies). All the streets in La Roseraie, where they lived, were named after flowers.

As soon as he got into the car, Michel, as usual, rolled down his window and lit a joint. Toni was now used to the smell and could pick it out anywhere in the streets. He turned the radio on, which was always tuned to "Radio Campus" where he was a part-time DJ.

Toni didn't like the radio station, but Michel never asked for her opinion, so she didn't say anything. After finding parking at the Catholic Institute's parking ground, they walked the few hundred metres to the restaurant. A waiter led them to a table in the corner of the room.

"The tables are so tiny," Michel began. "I'll come out of here with a broken back. Why couldn't you choose a better restaurant?" were his first words, as he removed his jacket which he used to dress the back of his chair.

A different waiter came and took their orders. Toni decided to taste the kangaroo. Michel went for a normal beef steak. Toni also asked for a glass of red wine. Michel asked for a Heineken.

"Michel," Toni began. "I have something to tell you. I've seriously thought about our relationship and I've concluded that it's not working out."

Michel opened his mouth to reply. Toni stopped him with a raise of her hand. "Let me finish ...." she begged. He sighed, set down his knife and fork, lifted his napkin from his laps and placed it next to his beer. He brought his hands up to cup his chin and looked at her.

"When I come back from Kenya, I'm going to leave you for good," she declared. "This relationship is not working. I want out," she added.

Michel turned pale and a tear rolled down one of his eyes. "Toni, please give me a second chance. I promise I'll try harder. Please don't do this to me," he begged.

Toni was taken aback by his reaction, which was completely unexpected. She had expected him to say something like, "Your loss, not mine." Michel had always made her feel as if she needed him more than he needed her but now he looked wounded, making Toni feel guilty for her harsh words. They left the restaurant in silence, their food half-eaten.

"Which radio station would you like to listen to Chérie?" he asked as soon as they entered the car.

Four years after leaving Kenya for France, Toni returned for a visit. She was apprehensive: Gone was the young Christian bride. In her place was a divorcee, co-habiting with a marijuana smoker.

When she descended from the plane, she was met by stifling heat, like a warm blanket that was suddenly thrown over her shoulders. It was February; the winter jacket and boots she had worn when she left Toulouse suddenly felt too heavy and cumbersome.

The sound of people speaking in Swahili and local dialects stirred up warm feelings within Toni. She had not realized how much she had missed hearing Kenyans speak.

"*Nikusaidie* Madam?" Can I help you? A man asked Toni, jolting her into the present.

Before Toni could reply, a uniformed guard showed up beside her and chased the man away.

"Leave her alone. This is our sister. Go and look for old *wazungus* to con."

The man, Toni later learnt, wanted her to give him cash in exchange for carrying her luggage. Old white people were expected to have a lot of cash.

When Toni reached the arrivals hall, family members, lovers and tour guides carrying placards with names scribbled on them stood waiting to receive a loved one or a client. Toni recognized the Abercrombie and Kent uniform that Edgar had worn as a tour guide. A wave of nostalgia swept through her body when she remembered how happy she had been to travel to France with the man she loved. Before she could feel more sad, she picked out her parents from the crowd.

Her father wore a heavy brown jacket despite the heat while her mother had wrapped a warm shawl around her. Toni remembered how the airport had always been considered "cold" and smiled to herself; they did not know what the winter cold felt like.

For the first time in Toni's life, her parents hugged her. It was brief and awkward. Displays of affection were rare in her family. Her parents had aged; they looked darker than she remembered them. Or was it the bulbs that seemed to give off a yellow glare, rendering the whole airport dull and gloomy?

Toni's father drove them from the airport, via Mombasa road, to their home in Thika, where the family lived. They had moved from Ayany Estate when Toni was a student at Kenyatta University. She was about to ask her father why he was driving on the wrong side of the road when she remembered this was Kenya, where vehicles were driven on the left side of the road.

"Let's pray," Toni's father announced, as soon as they sat down in the living room, catching Toni by surprise. She could not remember the last time she had been involved in prayer. As her parents bowed their heads in prayer, Toni looked around the living room. The photo of her parents' wedding hung on the wall. Next to it was that of Toni's wedding. She could not bear to look at it. The thought of a lecture from her father about her failed marriage filled her with dread.

Toni could not sleep that night. The bed was the same one she had slept in years before and the bedspread was her old pink one, but sleep evaded her. It was not only the pesky mosquitoes that threatened to come in through the netting that hung from a nail on the roof, but her bed was not in the right position. Her mother had placed the bed in the middle of the room, instead of pushing it against the wall, as Toni had done in the past. She dared not move the bed at such a late hour. She would have to wait for the morning.

She longed for a cigarette, but that was an abomination in her parents' eyes. She felt like an animal in a cage. An animal that had managed to escape the cage for four years but had walked right back into it willingly. How would she survive three weeks in her parents' house? She wished she could run back to France.

"Toni, what are you doing?" Her father screeched, his voice almost knocking Toni off the stool she stood on, her hand on the photograph taken on her wedding day, now hanging on the wall.

"I'm taking down this photo. Remember I got divorced?" Toni replied, without looking behind. The first thought on her mind when she got out of bed that first morning was to pull down the photograph.

"Put it back right now! This is not your house. I shall decide when I want to remove the photograph!" Her father roared back. Toni obeyed without asking any more questions. She did not understand why her parents wanted to put up appearances for the people who came to their home, but she knew pushing the discussion further was futile. The photograph would stay on the wall. She had not forgotten her father's stubborn streak.

Surprisingly, Toni's parents never brought up her divorce. They seemed happy to continue believing she was still married to Edgar.

Toni was excited to see her friend Alison after many years. Since graduating from Kenyatta University, Alison had landed a job as a bilingual secretary with PricewaterhouseCoopers. She was happily married to a banker. The marriage was blessed with two children.

"Wow! Toni, you've really changed! Why did you cut your hair?"

The two girls sat across each other in the same Wimpy restaurant Toni had gone to meet John Mark, years before. Toni ordered a plate of masala chips, two sausages and two samosas, much to the amusement of Alison because Toni was hardly an eater. True, Toni was still not much of an eater, but she had missed the taste of her favourite Kenyan food. She dug in with glee, washing it all down with a bottle of Stoney Tangawizi. The two young women talked as they ate. Toni recounted to Alison how her marriage had failed, her crazy relationship with Jean-Pierre and her life with Michel. She did not say a word about Marco, a married man she was enamoured of. Alison was still the good Christian girl who went to church every Sunday. She told Toni that most of their classmates from Kenyatta University had married and had children.

"Andy keeps asking after you," Alison said.

"Oh really?" Toni answered with more than passing interest. Isn't he married?"

"No. He isn't. I don't think he's in a relationship, either. You two really suited each other. It's a pity you left," Alison replied.

A few days later, Toni's phone rang. She recognized his voice immediately. She could even smell the "Azzaro" on him.

"Andy! How did you know I was around?"

"A little bird told me. Are you free this weekend? I'd really love to see you again," Andy replied.

The sound of his voice had the same effect on her as it had the first time she had met him: It left her breathless. She accepted to meet him the next Saturday.

"I'm going to visit Alison for the weekend," Toni lied to her parents.

After university, Andy had joined the Kenya Wildlife Services, where he now held a prestigious position in the conservation of endangered species.

Andy had a surprise for Toni. They drove all the way to the Maasai Mara, where he had reserved the most prestigious tented camp for the weekend.

As they sat at the fireplace, Toni remembered her trips with the Wildlife Club in primary school and the songs they sang around the bonfire. It all seemed so far away; so much had happened since then.

Being with Andy felt like the most natural thing for Toni. They were back in Kenyatta University, sitting on a bench outside the hostels, talking about themselves.

He told her how sad he had felt when she got married and flew out of the country soon after. There were so many things he would have loved to share with her.

"Why didn't you ask me to be your girlfriend when we were in campus?" Toni asked the question that had always bothered her.

"You were such a good, strict Christian that I didn't want to spoil you," Andy explained.

"But I thought you were also a Christian! I was horrified the day I found that girl in your bed. I didn't understand what was going on."

Andy laughed, "Toni, everybody was doing it. Couldn't you see?"

That night as they lay side by side on the big bed in the tent, Toni knew that the love of her life had slipped through her fingers.

They made love slowly, savouring the fragile moment, unwilling to trust in second chances. It was an experience like none Toni had had. It was wave after sweeping wave of untold bodily pleasure. Toni could not tell where one dose of pleasure ended, and the other began. It was too good to be true, and as her heavy eyelids finally gave in to the tranquility of the savanna night, Toni had the uncanny feeling that she would never feel this way again. Andy and the Mara would forever be etched in her heart. It did not matter if she never saw him again.

When Toni returned from her holiday in Kenya, Michel had completely transformed into a different person, a nice person. He did not spend all the time in his music room, he brought her breakfast in bed, bought her roses, and even gave her his old Renault 5 when he bought himself another car.

He seemed genuinely sorry, but something was wrong. When they tried to make love, Toni's body completely rejected him. Her vagina went dry every time he penetrated her, bringing back bad memories of her marriage.

Toni knew it was over between her and Michel; there was nothing she could do to love him again. The fact that Marco had also come into the picture further complicated the situation. In the weeks before travelling to Kenya, she had had several dates with Marco, behind Michel's back. It wasn't hard to cheat on Michel; she simply lied that she was going babysitting. Sometimes parents from Ma Première Page asked her to babysit their children in the evenings.

Michel was too busy with his music and weed to bother confirming where she went.

Toni would spend the evenings with Marco then come home to sleep on her mattress in the spare room. Three weeks after her return from Kenya, Toni moved out of the flat she shared with Michel. She had made up her mind to leave and leave she did.

Jessica took her in temporarily and did not even ask her to help pay the rent; which was a relief, because she was still paying her half of the rent for the flat she shared with Michel and would continue for three months. The lease demanded a three-month notice before vacating the house.

It was her first real date with Marco. He was taking her out for dinner.

"Please dress like a lady; no trousers please," he had instructed on the phone.

Toni had chosen a long, red skirt with a slit on the side; a lacy, black top; and chocolate-coloured pantyhose. She had learnt, from a fashion TV show that chocolate suited her skin tone better than black. She wished she had a sexier coat, but for now her old black coat would have to do. In the Metro on her way to town, she felt a bit nervous, but as soon as she saw Marco, she relaxed. She felt safe with him, yet she hardly knew him.

Marco had asked Toni to meet him in a bar in town called "Le Sylène." He had said they would have a drink before heading out of Toulouse to the restaurant. When Toni got to the bar, she spotted Marco immediately. He was standing at the counter, in a loose, black silk shirt with a small Chinese collar and almost invisible pinstripes. His shoes were shiny and pointed. He opened his arms as she approached, enveloped her in a tight hug and kissed her firmly on the lips.

"Bonsoir mon Bébé," he said in his deep, sexy voice, as he stepped back and looked at her from head to toe. "You look very beautiful."

His attention and gaze were unnerving; and for the first time in her life Toni felt shy. She could smell his perfume, which she later learnt was *"Habit Rouge"* by Guerlain.

Marco had a light, springy walk. Holding Toni's hand,

he whistled as he walked to his Jeep. He held the passenger door open for her before walking round to the driver's side and sliding in behind the steering wheel.

There was a packet of Philip Morris cigarettes on the dashboard. He took out one, tapped it against the wheel, lit it, and handed it to Toni. He repeated the gesture with a second cigarette, that he put in his mouth and dragged deeply. They were soon on the highway towards the outskirts of Toulouse, singing along to the smooth tunes of Sam Cooke playing on the CD player. As soon as he'd switched gears and the Jeep had picked up speed, Marco placed a hand on Toni's laps, gently caressing her left thigh through the fabric of her skirt. Toni was caught by surprise and almost gasped.

"Le Champêtre" was an old farmhouse that had been turned into a country restaurant. It was smack in the middle of a green field, with an artificial lake out front, where ducks were wading.

An elderly man ushered them in. He shook Marco's hand and pecked Toni on the cheeks.

"Monsieur Marco, I reserved your usual table, next to the fireplace," he announced, as he took their coats. They walked in to low lighting and soft music. There were a few other couples in the restaurant. As they passed their tables, Marco stopped to shake the gentlemen's hands and to kiss the ladies on their cheeks. He seemed to know everybody, Toni thought. As soon as they were seated, a waiter brought a bottle of Rosé to their table. He uncorked it, served Marco and Toni and placed the bottle back in its chilling bucket, which was full of ice cubes.

"Cheers Mon Bébé", Marco said, lifting his glass to Toni.

"How did the waiter know what we wanted to drink?" Toni asked.

"Because I always drink Rosé, Mon Bébé, and I come here very often."

Toni wanted to ask how he had decided that she also wanted Rosé, but there was an air of authority about Marco that made her keep her mouth shut.

He reached into his briefcase and took out a packet of cigarettes. He pushed them to Toni and said, "Please light me a cigarette, Mon Bébé'.

Toni wondered why he couldn't light it himself, but she took a cigarette out of the packet, lit it, and passed it to Marco.

"*Merci Mon Bébé,*" he said, putting the cigarette in his mouth. Toni felt special. Marco looked at her in a way that made her feel so feminine.

"Try the sirloin steak, I'm sure you'll love it," Marco suggested. Toni loved beef, but that evening, she couldn't eat. Her appetite had disappeared completely. Something strange was happening to her. Marco would cut bits from his steak and feed them to her, like one would feed a child, but she struggled to chew. Her throat felt tight, like something was blocking it.

It was refreshing for Toni to finally talk to a man who seemed genuinely interested in her. He told her he was married and had three daughters. Toni wondered what his wife thought about him taking a girl out for dinner, but she didn't ask. He asked about her family back in Kenya and about her brother.

He then leaned forward and said, "Give me your hands." He took her hands, covered them with his and blew into them.

The warm air seemed to travel all the way from her hands to her chest and stomach. Marco signalled for the bill. When the waiter brought the bill, Marco reached into the front pocket of his trousers and produced a wad of notes, held together with a big paper clip.

He peeled off a few notes and slid them into the bill holder.

"Let's go Mon Bébé," he said to Toni as he reached out for her hand.

"Bonne soirée Monsieur Marco, see you soon," the elderly man bid them goodbye.

Instead of driving to the highway, which would lead them back to Toulouse, Marco steered the Jeep off the main road towards a dust road that seemed to lead to a private compound. There was no house in sight, only bushes with a clearing in the middle.

"Bébé," he said with a smile. "Please go to the back seat," he instructed as he turned off the engine.

Toni obeyed without question. She opened her door and walked around to the back. Marco was peeing on the other side, with a cigarette burning in his mouth. He stubbed it out, opened the door, and entered the car through the second back door. He pushed her gently onto the seat and rolled up her skirt to her waist.

"Please, never wear these grandma stockings again. I want you to buy stockings that hold on by themselves," growled Marco.

"Who the hell does this man think he is?" Toni thought to herself.

Marco was already peeling off the pantyhose, down to her ankles. He then removed her shoes and buried his head in her pussy.

"Mmmmm," Marco groaned. He lifted one side of her red thong and placed the tip of his tongue on her clitoris. With slow, gentle movements, he began licking her up and down. Suddenly, he stopped and looked up at her.

"Close your eyes Bébé," he ordered.

Toni closed her eyes as Marco pushed her thighs together and removed her thong. He parted her thighs, hooked his elbows under her legs on either side, and continued licking her, this time with his tongue flat, as if he was lapping an ice-cream cone. The feeling was too strong for Toni to control; she held the back of Marco's head with both her hands and arched her body as all kinds of electrical impulses shot through her body in different directions. She had never felt anything like that before. Marco blew on her pussy as she climaxed, and gently caressed her thighs with his hands, at the same time.

Toni didn't care that this man was making love to her in the back of his car, like teenagers who had nowhere to go because they lived with their parents. She didn't care that it was in the open and that anybody driving by could stumble upon them. She didn't even care that a wild animal could suddenly appear from the bushes. She felt safe in this man's presence and she wanted him to continue doing what he was doing. His breath was warm on her skin and her whole body was tingling and twitching involuntarily.

He stopped and leaned back a little, to free his bulging penis which was already threatening to tear its way out through the zipper.

Without undressing her completely, he entered her with one swift movement, as Toni raised her pelvis to meet him. There was no space left in her, he filled her up completely, as he thrust into her with strong deep strokes. His eyes never left hers, even as they came simultaneously, as if their bodies were accustomed to each other after many years. Deep inside her, as tears rolled down her eyes, Toni knew that her life would never be the same again.

Becoming Marco's mistress had turned out to be like joining a cult.

The week after their first date, Marco said to Toni, "I want you to meet somebody, without me. Her name is Solange, she will tell you everything you need to know about me. She'll call you to fix a meet-up."

Toni was already under Marco's spell and would have done anything he asked her to. The meeting with Solange had taken place in a café in the centre of Toulouse.

Solange had simply said "Meet me at Le Caribé at 4.00pm, I'll be in a green dress."

When Solange walked into the café, Toni's heart skipped a bit. There was something eccentric about this woman who had been Marco's mistress for fifteen years. She had piercing green eyes and jet-black hair in a bob-cut. The conversation had been awkward, Solange had asked her questions to which Toni didn't have answers.

"Why do you want to be Marco's mistress? Do you know what it entails? And do you love him enough to obey him and always be submissive?"

Solange had explained that being Marco's mistress wasn't easy and that only a woman who loved him with all her heart could fit the role.

"You can't disobey him. You must light his cigarette and stir his coffee. You can't cheat on him. You must respect his wife and never go to Le Zenith if she is there. No wearing trousers or very sexy clothes. No pantyhose. Do you have any questions?"

Toni had been attentive, almost wishing she had brought a notebook to jot down all the rules involved in being Marco's mistress. She observed that Solange smoked Philip Morris, like Marco, and she made a mental note to herself to switch to that brand of cigarettes. She wanted to be like Solange; she wanted to be Marco's mistress for fifteen years.

After the interview, Solange and Toni had joined Marco for dinner, at Le J'yGo, a restaurant not too far from the café. Marco was standing at the terrace, chatting with the owner of the restaurant.

When the two girls arrived, he first kissed Solange briefly, on the mouth, saying "Bonjour Bébé", throwing Toni off balance.

He then turned to Toni and grabbed her firmly by the waist, kissing her deeply for a few seconds on the mouth. "*Bonjour mon Bébé*", he had said. Toni had noticed the "mon" when it came to her. This Marco was an enigma.

That evening, instead of pushing his packet of cigarettes to Toni, he pushed them to Solange, who lit up not only his cigarette, but Toni's as well.

"I still have a lot to learn", Toni thought to herself.

At some point during the dinner, Marco said to Toni, "Welcome to the cult my baby. You have been approved."

Two months after being approved by Solange, Marco moved Toni from Jessica's flat to one of the flats he owned. Located in the St Aubin area, right in the heart of Toulouse, it was a quaint, one-bedroom flat with an American-style kitchen and bar. Toni loved it because it was modern and airy. She still slept on a mattress on the floor, but this time round she wasn't running away from a man, it was her choice. She had read somewhere that sleeping on the floor was good for her back, and neighbours would never hear the creaking noise of her bed.

Toni was still working at Ma Première Page, and she still enjoyed spending evenings at Le Bagamoyo, but if Marco called her and asked her to go back home, or to wherever he was, she dropped everything and ran. At the beginning she saw him every week. He would call her during the day and leave a message on her phone.

"Bébé, I'll pick you up at seven-thirty for dinner."

After a few weeks, he stopped warning her and would call her in the evening, when she was at Le Bagamoyo having fun with her friends.

He would just say, "I'll pick you up in twenty minutes," and hang up.

Toni would leave her glass unfinished and run to her flat to freshen up her make-up, change into a dress or skirt and be ready before Marco arrived. He wouldn't be happy if she was late.

One time, around four o'clock in the morning, Toni was deep asleep on her mattress on the floor. The sound of her phone ringing woke her up with a jolt. She panicked. The only people who ever called her at such wee hours were her parents in Kenya. As she fumbled with the light switch on her side, she hoped everything was fine back home. Such early morning or late-night calls usually announced sad news, like the death of a family member.

"Hello," Toni whispered into the phone,

"Bébé, it's me," Marco's voice resounded in the silence of the night.

"I'd like you to come and join me. I'm at the Esmeralda discotheque. Be here in half an hour please."

Toni almost cried. For the first time since she met Marco, she considered disobeying him. It was 4am, for heaven's sake, on a cold winter night. It would be freezing out there. All she wanted was to curl back into her warm bed and sleep. Why did he want her to drive out at such an hour?

Toni wasn't allowed to ask Marco questions. She was expected to obey without saying a word. Dragging herself reluctantly to the adjoining bathroom, Toni splashed cold water on her sleepy face, put on some light make-up and went to her closet. Marco didn't allow her to wear trousers when she was with him, not even in Winter. She settled on a black woollen dress and black fishnet, self-adhesive stockings. They wouldn't keep her warm, but she wasn't allowed to wear normal pantyhose or thick leggings. It took her longer than thirty minutes to get to the Esmeralda. Toni hated driving in the night and her little car suffered from the cold. It struggled to start and pick speed.

"You're late, Bébé", Marco said, as he grabbed her by the waist and squeezed her.

Toni was glad she had obeyed. The smell of Marco's perfume, the feel of him against her, was worth driving in the dark on a cold winter morning. He was sitting at a table with his usual friends. One of them, Didier, a tall bald man with tattoos all over, had done time in prison, for bank robbery. He owned one of the most successful Cabaret nightclubs in Toulouse.

Toni stayed with Marco and his friends, drinking gin and tonic until six, when Marco decided they could go home to sleep.

"I have to be at the school at seven-thirty, Marco; I'm doing the first shift," Toni said, as they got into bed.

"Then there's no use sleeping. Let's stay up and you can go straight to work." Marco said, kissing her neck.

An hour later, Toni woke up in a panic. "Marco! It's already seven-thirty! Oh shit! I'll get fired today!" Toni screamed in panic, as she rushed out of the bedroom. They had fallen asleep and had forgotten to put on the alarm clock. Toni was in deep trouble; she was supposed to open the school! Her colleagues would only come in after an hour. Marco drove like a mad man to the school. Toni hadn't had time for a shower. She had hastily brushed her teeth and grabbed her handbag.

She stunk of alcohol and cigarettes; she hadn't even had time to remove her make-up. Three parents were waiting with their children outside the school when she got there. They had to go to work and couldn't leave their children alone. Toni apologised profusely as she fumbled with the key and let the children in. She was so ashamed of herself, she wanted the ground to open and swallow her up.

"Toni, you smell like a gas cylinder. What did you get up to last night?" Nathalie remarked when she came in for work.

Toni told her the truth and promised it would never happen again.

"Be careful, Toni. Remember what happened with Jean-Pierre. You don't want to go there again," Nathalie warned.

Jean-Marie lived alone in the flat opposite Toni's. An eccentric, sixty-year old man with a huge stomach, he wore several gold earrings on one ear. He was a colourful dresser: red silk shirts worn with black leather trousers and a huge gold chain around his neck, black pointed shiny shoes, or yellow moccasins. At first, Toni found Jean-Marie pleasant and accepted his invitations to have dinner in his house. It was not long before she started avoiding him.

Since Toni was dating Marco, a much older man, Jean-Marie assumed that Toni was ready to be seen in public with any older man.

"Toni, would you like to accompany me to a gala on Saturday evening? I'm required to take a date along and I don't have any."

Toni knew that Jean-Marie was gay because he had

told her, but she didn't want anybody to think he was her boyfriend. And what if they bumped into Marco at the gala?

"I'm sorry Jean-Marie; I don't want to bump into Marco," she had said as a polite way of declining the invite.

In her heart of hearts Toni was scared that Marco might appear at the gala with another woman. Toni could not live with that, mistress or not.

Jean-Marie grated on Toni nerves for his habit of feeding the stray cats that came into the building. Toni had told him of her phobia of cats, but he would still put a saucer of food outside his door for the cats. As soon as Toni opened her door, she would scream in fear if she found a cat eating the food. She resorted to always having a bottle of water near her door to pour on the cats.

Then she had what she thought was a bright idea: any time Jean-Marie was not at home, she would throw away the saucer of food he kept outside his door. But every day, the saucer became bigger and had more food. Toni was perplexed; what was going on? She decided to ask Jean-Marie.

"Hey, Jean-Marie, why have you increased the amount of food you give to the cats?" Toni inquired.

"Because they're finishing the food too fast," he replied.

Toni admitted that she was the one who threw away the food, which made Jean-Marie burst out laughing.

"I was wondering what was going on. You naughty girl! I'll start putting the food in the garage downstairs so that you don't have to meet the cats again," he promised.

Toni was excited because Marco was coming over for dinner; a very rare visit. He was a ruthless lover, who punished and rewarded Toni as if she was his prisoner. If she didn't pick his calls, he ignored her for up to two weeks and would only talk to her after she had left messages apologizing for not picking his calls. It didn't matter that she was like everybody else and sometimes didn't hear her phone ring or was busy elsewhere. When he called, he expected her to pick up on the first ring.

"I'll be there at 8pm. Don't make anything fancy," he had said. Toni was preparing one of her specialties: stuffed bell pepper and tomatoes to be served with plain, white rice. She had uncorked the bottle of Rosé that had been chilling in the fridge. Marco only drank Rosé with a lot of ice cubes. Toni made sure she always had a bottle in the fridge.

The bell peppers were boiling in hot water. When they were almost cooked, she removed them and let them cool before stuffing them with spicy minced meat she had prepared earlier. At exactly eight, the key turned in the lock of her front door and Marco let himself in, whistling, as usual.

"Come here Mon Bébé," he ordered, as he dumped his briefcase on the nearest sofa.

He was wearing a white silk shirt and black flowing pants. The smell of Habit Rouge, his perfume, filled the room. Toni ran to his embrace and put her arms around his neck, planting her lips on his.

"Switch off the cooker. I want to eat your pussy right now," Marco grunted.

As Toni walked to the open kitchen to execute the order,

Marco slapped her bum playfully. He was already undressing when she came back. Off came his black shiny shoes. His belt, too, releasing the pants to the cold floor. Toni undid his shirt buttons, removed the shirt and laid it on the armchair, without creasing it.

"Come here," Marco said, as he lifted her up in one sweep and took her to the bedroom.

He lay her on the mattress and lifted her knees.

"Good girl. You're not wearing any knickers. You're a very good girl," he said, grinning with pleasure at his own compliment.

He buried his face in her pussy and started lapping it up, licking it, blowing at it and sucking it. Toni closed her eyes and settled for what she knew were many minutes of pleasure. Marco could use his tongue and mouth on her pussy for twenty minutes nonstop.

When he came up for air, he asked "Whose pussy is this?"

"It's yours Marco," Toni whispered back.

"I didn't hear you; say it louder," he ordered.

"It's your pussy Marco," she said in a louder tone.

"Don't you ever forget that you belong to me."

Then he went back down and continued treating her to a heavenly delight.

"Do you want it now?" he finally asked.

"Yes, Marco, I want it."

"Then spread your legs wide to welcome him. He wants to get deep into you." Toni did as she was told and closed her eyes. Marco eased his thick dick into her wet pussy.

"Taste... taste him.... you deserve him," he moaned.

He gyrated his hips and pinned her shoulders down as he fucked her gently at first, then rammed her until she screamed, fucked her gently again, rammed her, the pattern going on until Toni couldn't hold it anymore. Just as she was about to climax, Marco pulled out without warning.

"Not so fast you greedy little bitch. You must give Marco his treat first."

Toni knew what that meant. Marco lay down on his back and Toni knelt in front of him, taking his erect cock into her mouth. He was warm and taut. Just the way she loved him. She started licking him the way he had taught her to; beginning with the vein that ran all the way from the base to the tip. She covered her teeth with her lips, so as not to hurt him, took his cock in one hand and, tracing him with her fingers, the shaft between the circle formed by her thumb and forefinger, she slid her hand up and down, as he grew harder. Her other hand cupped his balls delicately. After Toni sucked his cock for a few minutes, Marco reached down and lifted Toni onto him. He sat her on top of his cock and entered her with one smooth movement, making her gasp.

They moved in a synchronized motion, a deep tantric connection where their breathing was audible. He looked deep into her eyes as he pumped her, his hands exploring her small body. He kneaded her thighs and the feel of his strong hands on her further excited Toni. Her breathing was heavy, she felt like she was floating on a magic carpet.

"Are you ready?" he whispered. Toni nodded, too weak to talk.

As they climaxed at the same time, Toni, amidst tears

and sobs, clung to Marco.

"Marco, I belong to you. I'll be your slave forever, Marco," she declared.

Without answering, Marco stood up, lit a cigarette and walked into the bathroom. He took a few puffs as he looked at himself in the mirror. They then took a shower together, as they did every time after they made love. Marco always bathed her as if she were a small baby. He took the face towel and sprinkled some shower gel onto it. Then he scrubbed her whole body and rinsed her, before cleaning himself.

"Choose a nice dress, I'm taking you out for dinner."He had already forgotten that she had been preparing dinner for him. She didn't protest; she slipped on a soft, yellow dress and followed Marco to his Jeep.

When she wasn't at Le Bagamoyo, Toni went to "Le Gingembre," a pub, which was a five-minute walk from her flat. She liked the music there. What's more, she could rush back home if Marco called. She always sat at a corner with a book and a glass of Rosé, whiling away the evening, hoping Marco would call and take her out for dinner. When she was at Le Gingembre, a lot of men would try to chat her up, offer to buy her a drink, but Toni would always say, "My boyfriend will be here shortly."

If one became too insistent, she would finish her wine and go home, or go to Le Bagamoyo.

One evening, her old friend Remy, whom she hadn't met in years, walked into the pub.

"Remy!" Toni screamed.

"Toni! Long time!" he shouted back, kissing her warmly on the cheeks.

While locked in that reunion embrace, a young woman walked up to them.

"Toni, meet my girlfriend, Isabelle," Remy said.

"I know Toni. Hello Toni," the woman said, offering her hand. The woman looked familiar, but try as she might, Toni could just not remember where she had met her.

"Don't you remember me Toni?" she finally said. "I am Isabelle, Jean-Pierre's daughter."

Toni's eyes bulged in shock as the realisation crept in.

"Isabelle!" Toni finally managed. "Oh my God!" Toni gasped as she jumped to her feet to give her a hug.

Isabelle recounted how Jean-Pierre had fallen ill because of drinking too much, and had a heart operation, but was much better.

He had taken early retirement from the police. Léo had joined the police, like his father – as had Isabelle, much to Toni's surprise.

Marco often talked about Miriam, a girl he had dated for a few years before Solange. He said Toni's innocence and naivety reminded him of her. She had moved away to the United States but came to visit once a year. Toni was intrigued by this girl she had never met. Marco said she was of mixed race and that she was beautiful.

"The next time she comes to France, I'll introduce you to her.

I'm sure you'll get along very well," Marco had promised.

A few months later, Toni was at home, alone, dozing off in front of the TV. She was sad for she hadn't heard from Marco in a week. She still didn't understand why he kept disappearing from her. Surely, how long did it take to make a phone call, just to say hi? Suddenly, her phone rang. She looked at the time, it was almost midnight. Who could it be? She was now used to her phone ringing at weird hours because of Marco but the thought that it could be bad news from Kenya never really left her.

But it was Marco calling. Telepathy was in her favour, after all.

"I'm on my way with a friend," he said before hanging up.

Toni jumped out of the sofa and ran to the bathroom to freshen up. She quickly applied some eyeliner and lip-gloss, then slipped out of the jogging suit she wore when she was at home alone, and wore a simple, red dress. Marco would not be pleased to be received in a jogging suit. She also sprayed some perfume on herself.

Walking back to the living room, she put off the main light and switched on the side lamps that gave a warm, soft glow. She switched off the TV and inserted a Luther Vandross CD into the player. Toni always kept a bottle of chilled Rosé in her fridge. She uncorked it and placed three wine glasses on the coffee table.

She wondered which of his friends he was coming with. Maybe Christian, his business partner, whose girlfriend lived in the same building... or that crazy tattooed Didier. The key turned in the lock.

"Come in Bébé," Toni heard Marco say.

"Ah... he's with Solange. What a nice surprise," Toni thought. She admired and secretly envied Solange, who had a special place in Marco's life because she had been his mistress for longer than all the other mistresses he had had.

But it wasn't Solange. Before Toni's eyes stood the most beautiful creature she had ever seen.

"Bébé, please meet Miriam."

So, this was the famous Miriam Marco often spoke about. She was gorgeous. Toni couldn't tell if she was white or black. Her skin was golden, like a mixed-race person, but her eyes were blue, her short hair blonde. Toni would learn later that her father was from the West Indies and her mother was white. Miriam smiled gently at Toni and drew her into a tight hug, as if she were an old friend she hadn't seen in years.

"I'm so glad to meet you Toni, Marco has told me so much about you!"

Toni couldn't keep her eyes off Miriam, but she didn't want to stare either. She served them some wine and listened to their conversation. Miriam had a lot of stories to tell Marco because they hadn't met for a year.

"Shall we go to bed?" Marco said, catching Toni off-guard. She looked at Marco quizzically, with her eyebrows raised.

"Yes Bébé. Remember what you asked me? This is your present," he answered.

She hadn't expected this at all! It took Toni a minute to make out what Marco was talking about. Then she remembered: One night after one too many glasses of Rosé, she had said to Marco, "I wonder what a threesome feels like."

"Would you like to try?" Marco had replied.

"Yes," Toni had answered without thinking.

Marco lay down between the two girls, on Toni's mattress, one arm around each girl's neck. He turned his head to kiss each one, as he grunted in anticipation.

Watching Marco make love to Miriam was a revelation to Toni. She realized that she didn't know the man at all. Or rather, that her relationship with him was still very shallow. The way Miriam called out Marco's name... the way they were in sync ... She felt like a stranger who had walked in on a couple making love in the park, and all she could do was watch them, mesmerised at the beauty of it all.

Miriam was a dancer. She had a lithe and sensual body. Her breasts were just the right size. Toni suddenly felt ugly, too short. She wanted to cover her tiny breasts with her hands. She wished she could run out of the room. But she had asked for this and she was going to stick with it to the end.

When Marco had asked, "Are you ready?" as he always asked Toni, Miriam had answered, "Yes, my master."

Toni made a mental note of the response. When Miriam finally came, Toni slipped out of the bed and went to the living room to smoke. It was summer, the air was warm. She could hear noises coming from the bar downstairs. She couldn't decide how she felt. She wished she had never asked for this experience.

Marco came up behind her and held her by the waist. "You'll be fine, Bébé.... just trust me."

The following morning, Toni had to go to work. She left Marco and Miriam asleep in her bed. As she drove to Ma Première Page, her heart felt heavy. There was an ache she could not define. Toni imagined them making love all over again; she imagined Miriam whimpering and begging, "Yes, master..." She felt such a pang of jealousy, she feared it might kill her.

"Are you okay Toni?" Nathalie asked her the minute she walked into the school.

"I'm fine. I just had a sleepless night due to the heat," Toni lied.

It was the longest day of Toni's life. When she returned to her flat, Marco and Miriam had left. Marco did not call her for the next one week. This absence of communication from Marco made her life even more miserable.

After the experience with Miriam, Toni felt Marco withdrawing from her. He called less and stayed for weeks without coming to see her. Toni had accepted that she could never be like Miriam or Solange; she felt inferior and less beautiful. She started going out with her friends more, sometimes leaving her phone at home. Le Bagamoyo had changed locations, to a bigger and more modern building, just two streets away from Toni's house. She spent all her evenings there. George, however, did not approve of her chatting with other men.

"Toni, Marco wouldn't like that, you know. Be careful," George would warn her if she danced too close to a man.

"He's not my father. Besides, he's already married," Toni would reply, although deep in her heart she could not imagine her life without Marco.

George had become Toni and Ken's adopted father. So, it was not surprising for him to ask to speak to them as he did when, on a random day with Ken was working in the kitchen of Le Bagamoyo and Toni chatting with other customers, he summoned both to one of the empty tables.

"I have a business project in East Africa. I will be travelling to Kenya in a few weeks and while there would like to meet your parents," he announced.

Toni and Ken were excited; they wanted their parents to meet this man who had not only saved their lives by giving them jobs, but who also protected them like a father would.

True to his word, a few weeks later, George traveled to Kenya and met Toni's parents. They had heard so much about him that they insisted he stops paying for a hotel room and go and stay at their home. When George came back from Kenya, he felt even more like family.

"Please make sure you get permanent residency if you want to stay in France for a long time," he said to Toni and Ken. "Don't fool around. A lot of Africans come here and then get deported because they let their papers expire."

Toni was worried about her papers. She no longer had Jean-Pierre to help her renew her student visa and Nathalie had not been able to help her. She decided to talk about it to Marco.

"The mayor's secretary is a good friend of mine," Marco said. "Call her and tell her I sent you."

The secretary renewed Toni's student visa for a year, but she warned, "This is the last year you will be able to renew your visa as a student. You will either have to go back to your country or get married to a Frenchman."

Toni was shocked when she heard the last option, coming from a government official. When she told George, he laughed for long before asking, "How do you think people do it?"

Marco had acquired yet another discotheque. It was called "Le Bateau" (the boat), because it was a re-converted boat, on the Canal du Midi, an artificial canal which runs from the Mediterranean Sea to the Atlantic Ocean, from Bordeaux via Toulouse.

It was in this discotheque that Marco's birthday was being celebrated. He was turning fifty-four. Toni had been Marco's mistress for two years. It had been a roller-coaster ride; both exciting and scary.

When Toni walked into Le Bateau for Marco's birthday, she found him standing with his usual group of friends, plus Solange.

There were a lot of people in the boat that evening, all friends of Marco's. The discotheque had been closed to the normal public for the occasion. Champagne flowed freely and there was a buffet with all sorts of canapé bitings, both sweet and savory.

Toni spotted Ingrid, her old friend, at the counter,

working. Ingrid's dream had finally come true; she now worked for Marco, as she had always wanted. A few months into her relationship with Marco, Toni had persuaded him to give Ingrid a job as a waitress at his new discotheque.

Toni broke away from Marco and his friends and went to say hi to Ingrid. They chatted for a few minutes, reminiscing about old times. Then Toni walked back to join Marco. But when she got to the group, Marco and Solange were not there.

"Hey, Didier, where's Marco?" Toni asked.

She thought she saw Didier exchange a smile with Bruno, another friend, but if they had, it disappeared as fast as it had come.

"I think they went into Marco's office," Didier replied, pointing in the direction of a closed door at the end of the boat.

Toni walked to the closed door and rapped on it.

"Enter," she heard Marco's voice.

The sight that met her was one that Toni would never forget. She wondered whether to run out or shut the door behind her. Solange was kneeling in front of Marco, who was lying down on a sofa. She had his penis in her hand and it was obvious she had been giving him a blowjob.

"Would you like to finish him off, Toni?" Solange asked a shellshocked Toni.

"N-n-n-o-o-o-o.... tha-nk-s. I'll just watch," Toni managed to stammer.

"Give me your hand Bébé", Marco reached out to her.

He held her hand tight as Solange's head bobbed up and

down, sucking his stiff cock.

He climaxed with a low, deep, growl.

"Merci mes bébés," he gasped.

When Toni walked out of Le Bateau that night, she knew it was over between her and Marco. There was only so much she could endure. She loved him with all her heart and she knew that she could never have him all to herself. She had been ready to live with that, but her heart was too weak to go through another humiliating episode like the one she had just had to endure. Why had he purposefully chosen to hurt her so badly?

Tears rolled from her eyes as she drove her little old car back to her flat. She was shattered and in utter incomprehension. When she got to her flat, she only managed to remove her shoes. She cried herself to sleep, fully-dressed and still made-up. The man she loved so deeply had just shattered her heart into a million pieces.

"Toni why are you wearing a black mask?" Ken asked her one Sunday morning, after they had been partying at Le Bagamoyo.

"I've been getting horrible migraines and can't stand the light," Toni replied.

"You better see your doctor. That's not normal," Ken advised. Ken had moved to Paris after being accepted into a prestigious art school. He no longer worked at Le Bagamoyo because it was too far. Still, he often took the train down to Toulouse to visit his sister. They would spend the evenings dancing and drinking at Le Bagamoyo, then return to Toni's flat.

When the doctor checked Toni's blood pressure, she was surprised. "Your blood pressure is too high. I'll refer you to a cardiologist who will monitor it better," she pronounced.

After several tests and examinations by the cardiologist, the cardiologist discovered that Toni suffered from chronic high blood pressure and would be on medication for the rest of her life. She read up on the condition and concluded that the relationship with Marco had triggered it.

"I'll pass by your apartment this afternoon. We need to talk," Marco said to Toni over the phone, one day. She hadn't heard from him for over a month.

When he let himself into the flat as he had always done, Toni's heart did not skip a beat. She stood up from the sofa and went to kiss him. Instead of kissing her on the mouth, he planted a peck on her forehead, which surprised Toni.

"I guess it's over between us Mon Bébé," he said slowly, searching her eyes.

Toni nodded sadly, her eyes not leaving Marco's.

"Let me make love to you one last time"

They walked into the bedroom. Toni suddenly felt shy and didn't want to undress in front of Marco, who felt like a stranger. She decided to get it over and done with for the last time. He did not lick her as he had always done. Instead, he wetted his finger and shoved it into her dry vagina. Toni winced as she mentally prepared for what she knew would be painful penetration. She even knew how her vagina would feel when he Marco was done. The sensation of chilies in her vagina came rushing into her mind.

"Who is inside you?" Marco suddenly asked, reeling Toni back to reality.

"I don't know," she replied without thinking.

Smack! Marco drew back his hand and slapped Toni hard on her left cheek.

Why did the words "I don't know" trigger such anger in men? she asked herself, as tears rolled down her face.

Marco roughly pulled his penis out of Toni's vagina and stood up. Speaking between clenched teeth, he ordered her:

"I want you out of this apartment by the end of the month."

Chapter THIRTEEN

When it dawned on Toni that she was on La rue des Paradoux, a rush of nostalgia went through her body.

She had not been to this part of town in years. It held both sad and happy memories for her. It is here they had first lived with Edgar, after they walked out of Laure's house. She wondered how her life would have turned out if she had stayed married to Edgar. As Toni walked on the street lost in thought, a loud and familiar voice called out to her.

"Hey you! Even a snake can be seen in the desert! How dare you pass in front of my restaurant and not stop to say hello?"

Toni swung around, and her eyes immediately fell upon a black woman, shaking a rug in front of a restaurant. In a flash of memory, her eyes lit up. It was Hawa, the Malian woman who had run an African restaurant on the street.

"Oh Hawa, I'm so sorry," Toni cried. "I didn't think you

still had the restaurant," she apologised as she hugged the beautiful woman, admiring her long dreadlocks.

"Where did you think I went to?" sneered Hawa. "Come on in! Come and tell me where you've been all these years. Don't tell me you've gone all French and that you don't remember people. Where's your husband? Did you get children?"

Toni had no plans for that evening. She had just moved out of Marco's flat and was now renting a small flat on the other side of town. She hated going home. Her new flat was not as cosy as the one she had lived in before. Worse, stray cats were everywhere. She was lonely and unhappy.

Hawa served her a small glass of Ti-punch, a rum cocktail made with lime and brown sugar. Toni took a sip and let the liquid run smoothly down her throat, savouring the taste. Shortly after, Hawa served her a plate of her special Malian rice, setting off sensations of hunger in her stomach. Since the incident with Marco and Solange, Toni had lost her appetite and hardly ate. A cloud of sadness followed her everywhere. Hawa's rice tasted exactly like the rice she and Edgar had eaten on their first day in Toulouse, at Laure's house in Bagatelle.

A tall, bald, middle-aged man walked into the restaurant.

"*Bonsoir*," he said to nobody in particular.

"Hello Antoine," Hawa replied.

"I'm afraid all my tables are booked for the evening, except the space next to this young woman, if she doesn't mind sharing."

“No problem,” Toni said, noticing the orange sweater the man wore. It was rare to see a white man dressed in bright colours in winter. The orange brought out the man’s blue eyes, Toni thought to herself. He wore a golden wedding band on his left hand.

Antoine walked to Toni’s table and pulled out a chair opposite hers.

“Hello,” he began. “Does this young woman have a name?” he asked with a warm smile.

Toni looked at him and their eyes met. She felt a familiar tug at her heart.

“My name is Toni,” she said.

*** END ***

About the Author

Waithîra Francis was born in Nairobi, Kenya and now lives in Toulouse, France.

Printed in Great Britain
by Amazon